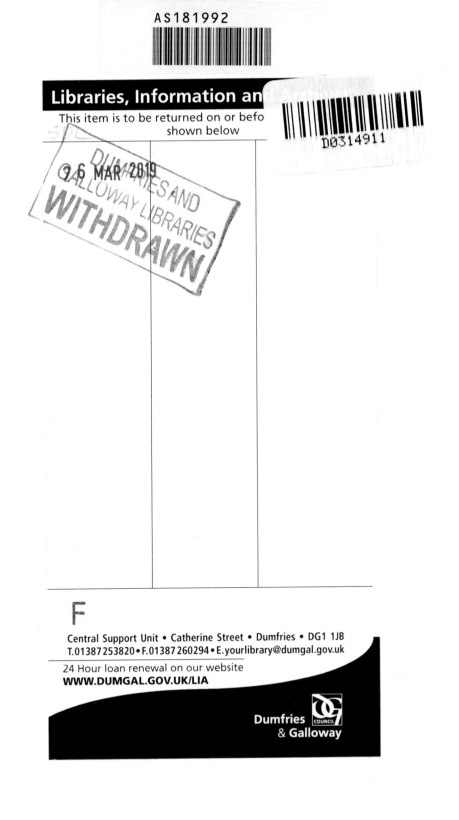

OURS, YOURS AND MINES

Living, loving and dying in the miners' rows
of Ayrshire, Scotland.
A family saga set in the mid-1800s to early 1900s.

Carmel McMurdo Audsley

ABOUT THE AUTHOR:

Carmel McMurdo Audsley is an Australian Journalist, Editor and Author who lives in Brisbane with her husband Iain. They both had Scottish fathers, share a mutual love of Scotland and have walked in the footsteps of their ancestors in the country that they love to visit. As a Newspaper Journalist and Magazine Editor, Carmel has written and had published thousands of news stories and feature articles and has now turned her research and writing skills to digging up the past and breathing life into the characters she finds.

Ours, Yours and Mines is her first historical fiction novel in a trilogy about the mining families of Ayrshire Scotland. Carmel now devotes all her writing and editing time to producing *Scots News Magazine* for ex-pat Scots in Australia, and researching and writing historical fiction.

Published by Theatricks Publishing, Australia.
theatricks@iinet.net.au

ISBN 978-1478102557

OURS, YOURS AND MINES

is dedicated to the men and women who lived and worked in the miners' rows in Ayrshire Scotland. Despite hardship and suffering, they lovingly raised their families to become decent, honest people who were not afraid of a hard day's work. Without them, many of us would not be here today. I also dedicate this book to my father, William Bell McMurdo, who was very much in my mind when I started researching and writing the book. Sadly, he passed away just a few months before he could hold this book in his hands. I think he would have enjoyed the story, and I hope you will too.

~Carmel

FOREWORD:

Growing up in Australia, I had always been curious about the country of my father's birth. My grandfather and cousins and aunts have visited us here in Australia, and we have travelled to Scotland, but it was the people who came before all of us that I was most curious about.

When I began tracing the McMurdo family history I found a long direct line of coal miners in Ayrshire, Scotland.

I felt a connection to the characters that I unearthed and wanted to find out about their lives. When I discovered that my great-great-grandmother, Mary Hamilton McMurdo, had borne eight children and buried seven of them, I was very upset and wondered how she, and the many women of the time who watched their children die, must have felt. I have heard some people callously say 'oh they expected their children to die back then' but, as a mother myself, I can't imagine that any woman would not be affected by losing a child.

I have visited the areas around Muirkirk, Hamilton, New Cumnock and Old Cumnock, where the McMurdo families lived, and researched life in the mid-1800s to early 1900s to form a picture of how life must have been. While the families who lived in the miners' rows suffered cramped living conditions, disease and death, there would have been good times as well and I wanted to illustrate that, but mostly they eked out a day-to-day existence.

This book is not a family history. It is an historical novel based on real people and places in the period 1861 to 1913 in the miners' rows of Ayrshire Scotland. The people are real and so are their circumstances and living conditions. All names of family members and neighbours, dates, and most of the events, are factual. I have put words into the mouths of my ancestors, and imagined their actions in some social situations. The prevalence of the names Thomas, George, Mary and Margaret can be confusing but it was the tradition to pass names down the family, as you will see in the story. The language used is English and Scots/English, the language of the people of the time, and the language I remember from my childhood growing up with a Scottish father. I felt it was important to give the characters a voice that was authentic. For Scottish readers, I hope I've done the language justice and for readers who are not familiar with some of the language,

I've included a list of Scottish words at the back of the book. Thank you to my cousins in Scotland for sharing information, photos and family anecdotes and to the new cousins in the UK and America that I met along the way.

The story begins with Thomas and Margaret McMurdo and their growing family and describes their simple lives crowded into a two-room dwelling in a miners' row. There are many highs and lows for the family. You will be introduced to their children, and particularly their eldest son George who (against her mother's wishes) marries 18-year-old Mary Hamilton, a carefree, educated young woman. If there must be a heroine in this story, then it is surely Mary for she is courageous and true in the face of great hardship.

You will read of the family's friendship with well-known union activist Keir Hardie. It's a story about the struggles of the miners and their families – the men who slaved away underground facing daily dangers, and the women who worked hard, bearing and raising large families and praying that their men would return unharmed from the pits. To tell you any more at this point, would spoil the story.

This is a story that relates to many people of the time. We often read statistics about the decimation of families due to disease, but there are few accounts of how the loss of family members, and the poor living conditions, must have affected them (particularly the women), emotionally and physically.

Ours, Yours and Mines is a tribute to them all.

Carmel McMurdo Audsley

CONTENTS

Chapter 1 (1861)

HOME AND HEARTH

In the early Summer of 1861, with a chill still in the air, coal miner Thomas McMurdo emerged from the dark, deep, gaping hole in the ground where he had spent the past ten hours. Covered in coal dust, he blinked his hazel eyes in the weak early morning light and breathed deeply of the cold crisp oxygen as he exhaled some of the stale air that had accumulated in his lungs. He lifted his worn, dirty cloth cap from his mop of straight, brown hair and rubbed his furrowed brow as he gazed at the mist that rose almost to the summit of Cairn Table, the hilly peaks that dominated the horizon, far away from the grime of his life in the miners' row. He had worked the nightshift at Linkeyburn pit at Muirkirk South, and though he was bone weary, he appreciated every shilling that he earned. Five years earlier when the coal miners in the west of Scotland had gone on strike to improve their pay, the men were without work for sixteen weeks and their families suffered greatly, some to the point of starvation. Thomas and the other miners were paid for every tub of material they sent up to the head of the pit, but payment was subject to the quality and weight of each tub, and also to the judgement of the coal owners' representative called the Banksman as to what the miner would be paid. Many a miner toiled at a hard day's work only to find that the Banksman had condemned some of his tubs and his pay was lessened accordingly. Shifts available were also at the mercy of the coal mines' owners and some of the men willingly worked double shifts to improve their pay.

Although just 45 years of age, the upper half of his 5ft 9 inch frame was already slightly stooped from nearly 30 years spent working in confined spaces underground, mining coal. Muirkirk, about 10 miles from Douglas in Ayrshire Scotland, lay between the rivers Doon and Irvine and was a bleak and dreary place with a landscape of treeless moorland hills, with the higher grounds clothed in a dark-coloured heath. Its rough mountainous territory had become part of the great coalfield of Scotland producing coal, ironstone and limestone, and the murky smoke from the coal pits and furnaces only added to the cheerlessness of the countryside. Thomas's work as a coal cutter was hard, cutting coal by hand in narrow confined spaces sometimes barely 18 inches high, but there was little choice of employment and no plan for the future. He and the other coal miners were defined by their surroundings, with little time for anything except long hours of hard labour, but his needs were simple. The thought of heading home to his wife Maggie and the weans, the warmth of the fire in his crowded little house and breakfast in the pot, made him smile.

He started the short walk along the crushed dust road, with its large ruts made by the constant traffic to the pits, to his home at 27 Linkeyburn Square. As each new pit was sunk, the mine owners built basic houses near the pits so that the men and their families would be close to work. Transportation was limited and most people walked wherever they needed to go. The closer the men lived to their work, the higher the attendance rate and therefore the more coal and profits that came out of the pits.

The housing became known as miners' rows as they were usually built in rows to save materials and space, and were huddled together near collieries. The mining families formed their own communities as the rows and the pits were usually located in the countryside, away from major villages.

The dark brick buildings of Linkeyburn Square had been built by the mining company belonging to William Baird and Co to accommodate the miners and their families, and the rows were a familiar sight at mines across the Ayrshire countryside as the need grew for coal to be extracted out of the ground. Ayrshire produced coal for household use, factories, the blast furnaces of Glengarnock, Kilwinning, Stevenston, Waterside, Lugar and Muirkirk, the locomotives of the Glasgow and South Western Railway and for export to Ireland through Ardrossan, Troon and Ayr.

Thomas and his family moved from mine to mine and followed the work. They had lived in the miners' rows of Glenbuck and Wellwood Row with thousands of people, but Linkeyburn Square was smaller by comparison with only 15 two-roomed houses set out in a square. Each dwelling was little more than four walls, two windows (if you were lucky), a door and a slate roof covered with soot and coal dust. Most houses were kept clean inside and out, and only as cosy and welcoming as the cleanliness and efficiency of the individual coal miners' wives, but the habits of a few untidy women could spoil the whole look of the rows. Perhaps their lack of care stemmed from the transiency of their tenure for they lived from week to week, dependent upon the mine owners for their pay and a roof over their heads. To some of the women of the miners' rows, the dwellings would never feel like home and they didn't put a lot of effort into their upkeep, while others took great pride in making a cosy atmosphere for their families.

The kitchen of the modest dwellings measured 15 feet by 10 feet, and the other room – the bedroom or hole in the wall - measured 11 feet by 6 feet. The McMurdo family, like the other families who lived in the miners' rows, were packed into their little house like sardines in a can. Side by side, same upon same, the little dwellings with their compacted earthen floors and whitewashed interior walls provided basic shelter in two rooms for the large families that called them home.

There was always a plentiful supply of water flowing through pipes fed from the hills into the open drains about 9 feet from the door of each house where the women collected water for washing and cooking. Over 100 tenants crammed into the 15 little houses and shared three coal houses, with coal provided as part of the miners' earnings, and a few dry closets with open ashpits the only form of toilet facilities. The stench from the dry closets in Summer was sometimes unbearable.

Thomas's workmates and neighbours walked at various speeds along the unpaved path – some anxious to get home to a welcoming fire, others dawdling along to postpone the reception they would receive. While they shared their work and living conditions, not all the men had the love of a good woman waiting for them at home.

"Will we see ye at The Black Bull later Tam?" asked Thomas's neighbour James Regans as they walked along.

"Aye, ye will at that," replied Thomas as he continued trudging along the road. A few drinks with work mates was one of the few pleasures known to the men of the mining community – it helped numb the physical aches and pains brought about by working in cramped, dusty conditions. While some men took the drink too far, spending more at the Black Bull than their wives had left to buy food and provisions, most of the miners valued their self-reliance and respectability and drank in moderation, but drinking was a problem in many mining communities – no doubt about it.

When Thomas reached the stoop of his home just after six o'clock in the morning, the miners' row was quiet. At that hour, no children were playing in the streets, and there were no horses' hooves making dull, crackling sounds as they pulled carts along the coal-strewn streets. All that would come with the full light of day. For now Thomas enjoyed the peace as he opened the door to the two-room but 'n' ben he shared with his beloved Maggie and their eight children. The two youngest Davey, 3, and five-year-old Rab were still fast asleep as they lay in the bed they had shared with their mother during the night, but the rest of the household was bustling. The middle children Elizabeth, 7, John, 9, and Jimmy, 12, were up getting ready for school while the older lads George, Thomas and William, born in that order, prepared to go to the mine on the dayshift.

The smell from the fire invaded Thomas's nostrils as he paused to take in the familial scene. Across the room stood his beloved Maggie, the lynchpin that held the family together. Her short, ample figure was stooped over a large pot of porridge bubbling over the fire, her swollen belly tight beneath her faded grey, floor-length dress and brown calico apron, and the strands of her long golden hair already working loose from the neat bun she had fashioned when she rose from her bed two hours earlier.

She paused from her morning duties to see the tired, blackened face of her husband, and threw him a smile across the din of their noisy brood as everyone prepared for the day ahead.

"Away to the wash-house Tommy," she called as the loving smile faded from her face. "Yer breakfast is ready for the eating." To his workmates and friends Thomas was known as Tam, but to Margaret, his Maggie, he was her Tommy.

"Hello faither," said Elizabeth. "Did ye have a good shift?"

"Aye, lass, all is well," was Thomas's usual reply. It was comforting for all to hear. For Elizabeth, it was reassuring to know that her father's work was safe, even though the truth of the matter was quite different. For the older boys it meant that there had been no accidents underground the night before, and nothing immediate to be concerned about. Mining was a dangerous occupation, not only because of the ever-present fear of injury, but also for the ongoing health problems caused by damp and breathing in coal dust. For the most part it was steady work as the need for coal increased to feed the progress that the industrial revolution had brought to Britain, but injury, unemployment or the death of a coal miner often meant destitution for the families.

As Thomas made his way out of the kitchen, through the hole in wall to the bedroom and out the back to the wash-house, wee Lizzie (as Elizabeth was known to the family), with long golden hair like her mother, struggled to carry a porcelain pitcher of warm water to the bench outside. Placing it gently on the wooden bench, she quickly ran back to the kitchen to fetch the soap and towel which she handed to her father to wash off the remains of his working night. Thomas poured the water into the large tin basin and dipped in the cloth, aware that his young daughter had not moved from his side. She had seen him covered in coal dust every day of her life, but she always seemed to marvel at the transformation removing the black remains of his working day made to her father.

"Is that a spot of soot on yer nose there Lizzie?," her father chided her as he brushed his own blackened finger across her nose and left a sooty smudge on her tender young skin. "Have yer brothers been using ye to sweep out the chimney again, lass?"

She giggled and squirmed and laughed so hard that she could not answer. Finally she replied in her sweet, seven-year-old voice: "No faither. I've been doon the coal mine watching over ye in the night and I got a wee speck o' dust on my face."

Faking anger, Thomas replied: "My wee Lizzie will no be doon any dirty old coal mine. She'll be a fine lady with ribbons and lace." Then softening his voice and whispering in her ear he continued: "but I thank ye for thinkin' o' me lass", and with that he continued to scrub the dust from his body while Lizzie skipped off back to her mother's skirt. Even when Thomas was dead tired, he always had the energy to play a game with his darling daughter. After five sons in a row, there was great rejoicing when Lizzie was born. And when two more sons followed her, she became even more precious to her doting father. Nothing was too good for his Lizzie.

The older boys George, Thomas and William were dressed and seated at the table tucking into their porridge as Lizzie helped her mother prepare their piece boxes to take for the day. Rats roamed the mines looking for scraps of food and the metal piece box kept the miner's sandwich clean. Most of the men also took a tea and sugar box with them each day to make a brew that helped wash down the dust.

Lizzie was a great help to Maggie, especially as the new baby was due any day now. Maggie prayed for another daughter to help her around the house. Four men working in the mines meant long hours spent over a washtub and with another six mouths to feed, and one on the way, the rest of her time was spent over the cooking pot. Her days began early and ended late and her energy was always sapped, but they were all in good health and the wages of four men in the house meant that they ate well and were well shod. It was a happy, if somewhat cramped, household.

Overcrowding in the miners' rows was a big problem but Thomas, Margaret and their eight children didn't seem to mind being squeezed into two rooms. The kitchen was the heart and soul of the house with a large fireplace that was kept lit 24 hours a day, over which hung a hook holding a big pot of porridge or stew, depending upon the time of the day. On another hook hung a kettle always filled with water ready to make a pot of tea. Clothing was hung in front of the fireplace to dry or hoisted above the fireplace on a wooden rack to help save space. On the mantle over the fireplace sat the clock that had been a wedding present from Margaret's parents, plus a set of candlesticks and candles from Thomas's parents, and the family bible that was updated each time a new child arrived. The well-used fire tools sat beside the hearth next to the coal basket and scoop, and in front of the fire sat two large arm-chairs which were used when guests visited and where Margaret did her needlework and knitting, and Thomas read the paper and told stories to the children. Her sewing skills, learned at the hand of her own mother, Elizabeth McCrone Stevenson, had come in handy and the house was dotted with hand-made doilies and blankets. To the left of the fireplace was a large oak dresser with a set of eight plates, pudding dishes, cups and saucers that had seen better days, two ashets and various mismatched pieces of cutlery. Next to the dresser was a small cupboard that Thomas had built to house staple ingredients such as potatoes, turnips, onions, flour, oatmeal and sugar.

Also in the kitchen were two box beds built into the wall, each fitted with a cover full of feathers. George, 21, Thomas, 19, and William, 16, shared the larger bed and their sister Lizzie shared the smaller bed with her brothers James, 12, and John, 9. Through the hole in the wall was the bedroom where Margaret and Thomas slept on a larger bed and the two wee boys, Davey, 3, and Rab, 5, slept on another box bed. The cradle for the new baby had already been placed beside the large bed in readiness. Through the back bedroom door was the makeshift wash-house and coal store. One outside dry toilet was none too private and used by four large families.

Despite the cramped quarters, the McMurdo family made do and Margaret had the household running like a well-oiled machine.

Breakfast over, the older lads grabbed their piece boxes, took their coats and caps down from the row of pegs by the door, shouted a general goodbye, each in turn kissing their mother on the cheek, and were off to work. Lizzie helped her mother clear the dishes and set the table as the younger boys Davey and Rab stirred from their bed. Thomas, now clean for another few hours, scooped them up in his arms and carried them to the breakfast table. Lizzie, James and John joined them for a quick bowl of porridge before they were off to school.

"Mind ye get some good learnin' today," their father called after them as Lizzie and James rushed out the door.

"I don't want to go to school today faither," cried nine-year-old John who was lagging behind his brother and sister.

"Stop yer greetin' and get off to school lad," his father said sternly.

Lizzie, two years younger than her brother John but many years wiser, took him by the hand and led him out the door.

The house was suddenly quiet as Margaret placed a steaming pot of tea on the table and sat down to her own breakfast with her husband and her two youngest children. Her face looked pale and drawn, and after giving birth to eight children already, at age 40 she wondered when her child-bearing days would be over.

"This child is on its way, Tam," she said softly.

"Are ye sure Maggie?," Thomas said with an air of concern. "Ye've got some time to go."

"I've had the pains since early this morning. This day our ninth child will be born Thomas McMurdo," she said flatly to her weary husband. "But never you mind about it now. Finish up and get to yer bed – ye must be exhausted from working all night."

"Aye, that I am. You'll wake me, mind, if ye need me?"

"I couldnae do it without ye," she said with a mischievous wink, and her husband knew she wasn't just talking about the birthing. They brought each other comfort during the long, cold winter nights and felt blessed as each new child came to them, even though it meant Thomas had to work harder in the mines, and Margaret always seemed to have one child on her and one child in her as she toiled with daily chores.

Margaret settled the wee boys with some wooden blocks on one of the box beds in the kitchen as she washed the breakfast dishes in a bowl at the table. Her oldest son George had fetched water from the open water drain early that morning to save her lifting the heavy buckets.

Her husband Thomas slept and as their household settled into its natural daily rhythm, the road outside their home began to fill with little children playing and women hanging washing in the weak sunlight. It was still early, just 9 o'clock in the morning, and Margaret had bread to bake and a stew to get on. The children would be home from school for their dinner at noon and the older boys would be home from the day shift around four o'clock. But the pains were more regular and she knew the signs. She walked quietly to the blanket box at the foot of her bed and took out the birthing sheets which she'd used for each of her children's births then boiled and pressed and returned to the chest after each use.

"Rab," she said softly to the five-year-old who'd been playing quietly with his three-year-old brother. "I want ye to run next door to Mrs Regans and tell her the baby's comin'."

Rab looked at his mother with wide eyes? "Will we have another little brother mither?", he asked.

"Could be, Rab, could be. Now on ye hurry to fetch Mrs Regans."

Rab scampered to the big wooden door and pulled it open with all his might then ran as fast as his little legs could carry him the few paces to the next door that was Margaret Regans' house.

He knocked with his tiny knuckles on the door and as it slowly opened he looked up into the ruddy face of the roly-poly Mrs Regans. Rab began tugging on her apron.

"It's me mither," he cried. "She says for ye to come!"

There was no midwife on the miners' row and rarely was a doctor called to a birth in this part of the country. The women were all experienced in childbirth and helped each other, with varying outcomes. The infant mortality rate was high, mostly due to the poor nutrition and back-breaking work of the mothers, and every live birth was cause for celebration.

By the time young Rab returned with Mrs Regans, Thomas had been awakened and the birthing sheets were on the bed. While clean, the sheets bore witness to each of Margaret's previous births and it was for two reasons that she kept this same set of sheets for this specific purpose – one to save her other linen from staining and also because she felt it linked each of her children together. The sheets were the first material thing that each of her children touched as they slipped from her body.

Margaret's pains grew stronger but she stifled her cries so as not to frighten the two wee boys.

"Oot now Tam," ordered Mrs Regans, "and take the wee lads wi' ye."

"I hope it will be quick for ye, lass," Thomas said to Margaret, then he took the boys by the hand to wait outside the house.

The birth path was well worn and the labour quick. Mary McMurdo made her entrance into the world at 10am on June 15, 1861. Her hearty cries could be heard outside the house as Mrs Regans emerged from behind the closed front door.

"It's a day fer rejoicin' fer sure, Tam," she said to Thomas who was sitting on the stoop. "Ye have a wee lassie as bonnie as any I've seen."

"A lassie," Thomas said softly, almost in disbelief. "Won't our Lizzie be pleased."

"A lassie!," cried Rab in disbelief. "A lassie! Me and Davey wanted a wee brother, did we no' Davey?" Wee Davey nodded his head dutifully, not caring either way.

"Ye can see yer daughter now, but I've yet to wash her," cautioned Mrs Regans.

As Thomas and the boys entered the bedroom, Margaret was cradling her new-born daughter. "We'll call her Mary, after yer

17

mither," Margaret said to her husband as she handed him the child wrapped in a sheet.

Their first child George, born 21 years before, had been named after Thomas's father, with their second son named after Thomas himself. Their first daughter Elizabeth had been named after Margaret's mother and the other boys were named after various relatives. It was that way in most families. As Mrs Regans got about washing baby Mary and tending to the child's worn-out mother Margaret, Thomas took the family bible down from the mantle place and carefully entered his daughter's birth details, as a warmth spread within his chest.

At noon Lizzie, James and John were home from school for their dinner and as they burst through the door they heard the baby's cry and rushed to the bedroom.

"It's a girl our Lizzie," said her mother, "a wee baby sister."

Lizzie's eyes were wide as she held out her arms to hold the infant. "A wee sister of my very own. What shall we call her mither?"

"She's Mary after your Granny McMurdo, just as you are Elizabeth after your Granny Stevenson."

"Oh, that's perfect mither," Lizzie said as she gazed down at her longed-for sister, while James and John looked on with idle curiosity.

While the children greeted their new sister, Mrs Regans had gone home briefly to collect her smallest children - four-year-old Mary and one-year-old Hugh – together with Margaret, 11, James, 9, and Jean 6 who were also home from school. She sat all the children down at the table with mugs of warm milk and bread and jam then shushed them out the door like a flock of chickens, back to the school yard.

"I'll make sure there's something in the pot when yer brood returns from work and school, Tam, and get yer piece box ready for the night shift. The sheets are changed so on ye go back to yer bed wi' yer wife and baby and I'll keep the weans busy."

Mrs Regans' husband James, who had been on the night shift with Thomas, slept while she bustled back and forth between her household and the McMurdos to organise pots of stew for both families. 'There'll be no bread baked the day', she murmured to herself, 'but there'll be plenty of tattie scones.'

Thomas awoke around four o'clock from his second attempt at sleep and kissed his wife and daughter on their foreheads as they slept. He headed off to meet his workmates and neighbours at The Black Bull, as previously arranged. But now he had more of a reason for a wee dram. He had to wet the baby's head and as he started down the road to the inn, he turned to see his sons George, Thomas and William coming home from the mine. He raised his arm and beckoned them to him.

"Dinnae bother washin'," he called. "Yer comin' straight to the inn wi' me. You have a sister called Mary and her head needs wettin'." The lads shook hands with their father each in their turn then the youngest William hesitated.

"Will I no' get in trouble for drinkin' faither?," asked the shy 16-year-old.

"What kind of trouble Will?," asked his father. "From the law or frae yer mither?," he chided his son as the others laughed. Will dropped his head in embarrassment.

"They might have changed the law up in London for ye to be over 16 to take a drink, but you're a workin' man son, and you're entitled to a wee drap now and then."

So it was settled and all the McMurdo men were back-slapped as word spread about the birth. Not that the birth of a baby was anything new in the miners' rows in and around Muirkirk, as there was a baby born every other week somewhere in the villages and rows, but it was always a joyous event in an otherwise humdrum existence, when a child was born hale and hearty, and it called for celebration.

When they reached the inn, there was a collective cry of congratulations as Thomas was handed whisky after whisky. He still had to work the nightshift but he gratefully accepted each drink as it was handed to him, and stumbled home with his lads around half past five.

George, Thomas and William who had celebrated a little less than their father, in turn poked their head through the bedroom door to greet their mother and gaze at their wee sister asleep in her cradle.

After supper, Lizzie helped Mrs Regans with the dishes then the family went about their usual routine – the older boys heading off to a friend's house for a game of cards, Lizzie, James and John practising their handwriting and arithmetic and Rab and Davey knocking down the blocks they'd built up during the day. Just before seven o'clock, Thomas left for his night shift at the mines, still feeling the effects of his session at the inn but he knew his mates would look after him. Alcohol and dangerous working conditions were not a good mix, but they were a good lot of men and looked out for each other. He would be all right. He had somehow managed to put out of his mind that just two days before, a miner on the day shift at his pit had his chest crushed when a large piece of coal suddenly came away and fell on him, breaking four of his ribs. Or that another miner at the same pit dislocated his thigh bone and had to be carted away by the doctor and have the bone pulled back into place. The miners faced danger every day they turned up for their shift. Earlier in the year a miner had been indulging rather freely in intoxicating liquor, and went to the pit-head under the influence, and at the pit-mouth he stumbled and fell 80 fathoms to the bottom of the shaft, mangling his body as he fell to his death and leaving a widow and two small children. The miners knew the dangers, but they tried not to think about it. So off Thomas went up the familiar dirt road to the mine to earn another night's wages to feed his family.

Margaret's dreams that night were full of her new baby and of her older boys George now 21 and Thomas 19. One day in the not too distant future, they would be leaving home to start families of their own but for now they were still all together, and she was happy.

The next day, Margaret was back at the helm, with a baby at her breast and two wee boys about her apron strings. The birthing sheets were washed, pressed and folded, and as she placed them back in the blanket box she wondered if she would need them again.

Chapter 2 (1862)

NEW LIFE AND ROMANCE

In May 1862, the cleaned and pressed birthing sheets were once again being placed back into the blanket box, with new stains added. Margaret Stevenson McMurdo was born in the same place her sister had been born just 11 months before. Named after her own mother, wee Margaret was placed in the cradle beside her parents' bed, and baby Mary, not yet one, slept with her parents in the double box bed, while Davey and Rab continued to share the other bed in the room.

The tiny bare-floored two-room house was full to the brim with five adults, five children and two babies. Margaret darted in and under nappies hung above the fire to dry as she went about her ever-increasing daily chores. Her days revolved around her husband's and sons' shifts at the mine. She would be up before them preparing their piece boxes to take to work, and ready with a meal for them when they came home. In between times, there was the never-ending task of keeping the house clean in a village clouded in dust and grime from the pit. Each housewife in the row took a turn at stoking the fire under the boiler and plunging first the household linen in to be stirred by a large wooden pole, and when they were removed, the children's clothes were washed, followed by the dirty pit clothes. While the babies slept, and the children played with each other, their busy mothers toiled day in, day out, without complaint.

The older boys George and Thomas talked of moving out to board with friends but they knew that their mother needed their wages and it was for this reason that they stayed at home. There was no privacy in the house and with only a wash-house out the back and an earthen closet some walk from the house that was shared with other families, it was a crowded, basic existence.

Sunday was the only day of rest for the miners. Their lives revolved around work, family, drinks with workmates and – reluctantly for some of the men – being seen to be an active member of the Church of Scotland. The church was central to most people's lives in Scotland, and exerted influence over the congregation through ministers who set the standards for daily living and warned of dire consequences if their ministering was not followed. The McMurdo family's Sunday began with a walk to the Muirkirk Church then home for a big family dinner as it was the only time that they could eat together. The adults sat at the large table, the babies were held and the children sat on stools that Thomas had built from scraps of timber. While meat didn't always feature on the dinner table, with the wages of her husband and sons Margaret managed a Sunday dinner of mutton, tatties, neeps, carrots, peas and gravy followed by a cloutie dumpling and custard or steamed pudding. She had a knack for making the money stretch.

The two eldest boys, George and Thomas, often contributed to what was on the table. The muirs afforded a great store of wild fowl such as the heath-cock and heath hen, partridges, green and grey plovers, ducks and drakes, and at the very least, hares. They would often go out trapping to help put meat in the pot. It was during one of their hunting trips that George confided in his brother Thomas.

"I've a mind to move out on m' own, Tam," he said as his brother busily set the snare.

"Aye, I feel it's come time for me to move on as well Geordy, but I've nowhere to go. Have you?," he enquired as he continued with the task at hand.

"No," he replied dejectedly, then continued. "You'll no tell anyone this, but I have m' eye on a lass in the village. She's no decked out in frills and lace and she doesnae bat her een at every lad who passes like some of the lasses, but I've set m' cap for her."

"Who is it Geordy?"

"Her name's Mary Hamilton and she works on a farm. Her family had a farm but things were no doin' so good, so her faither's taken to stone quarrying and Mary's taken on working at a neighbouring farm. I've seen her in the village. She's a good strong lass and has a good heid on her shooders an' all. She walks so tall and proud. I think we'd make a good match."

"Well, I wish you luck Geordy," said Thomas. "When do we get to meet her?"

"Soon, Tam. I've yet to mention anything to anyone – including Mary Hamilton," George said almost as an afterthought. They both laughed and frightened away a partridge that had been approaching the snare, but two hours later they were on their way home with three ducks for the Sunday dinner.

Lizzie, now aged 8, was busy helping her mother with the chores and taking care of her two baby sisters Mary and Margaret. On Sunday evenings, it was also her job to oil up her father's and her brothers' boots ready for the working week. She didn't have the knowledge to mind how hard she worked, for she knew it was expected of her. Besides, how else would her poor mother cope if not for Lizzie's help. It was the work of the men to bring in the money, and the work of the women to feed and clothe the children, look after the men and scrub and clean. They knew what was expected of them and, although they may have daydreamed in the odd, spare idle moment, no one complained and they just got on with the business of living.

With the wages of four men coming in each week, the McMurdos were better off than some in the miners' rows. The men had two sets of work clothes each and two sets of going out clothes. The work clothes were hung on pegs in the tiny wash-house after each shift and worn the next day and the next. Then, on her allotted wash day, Margaret would draw water from the community water drain and boil and scrub the clothes and hang them by the fire to dry. In Summer, she might get some sunshine and the washing would be hung on lines across the street with everyone else in the row's washing. The men's clothes and most of their tools, kitchen utensils and some food items were purchased from the company store set up by the mine owners. The prices were a little more than if they were bought in the nearby village in Muirkirk, but the miners and their families had no transportation and it was easier for them to buy from the store. The mining company of William Baird and Co owned their houses and rent was taken out of the miners' wages each week. After rent and food, Margaret saved any extra money in a small stone jar she hid in the food cupboard. Each week, Thomas and his sons would hand over their wages to Margaret who doled out an allowance for each of them to buy their tobacco and whisky or ale. Clothes were patched and handed down from one child to the next and on special occasions, Margaret would take Lizzie into Muirkirk to visit the shops and buy new aprons and bonnets or trousers for the boys. Lizzie loved these rare moments alone with her mother, away from the noise and work of home. Life outside the miners' row was a little different and Lizzie loved to watch the people go about their daily business as shopkeepers, blacksmiths, bootmakers and bakers. To her, the air seemed cleaner in the village, although that was unlikely as Muirkirk was surrounded by coal mines and iron works. Perhaps it was that there was more to see in the village and she loved the different sights and sounds. Occasionally, her older brothers would give her a halfpenny for oiling their boots. She'd save up her money and take it on their shopping trips and come home with sweeties for herself and Davey and Rab. As she stopped to look in the window of a bookshop, she daydreamed about owning a brightly-coloured picture book that she saw propped up on a chair.

"Do ye think I could have that book for Christmas, mither?," she enquired as she brushed a golden curl from her face. Margaret looked down at her daughter, knowing her love of books and learning and wondering what use it would be to her, for her life's path was planned out before her. Lizzie would marry a coal miner, live in a miners' row and have babies and look after her family. But she saw the light in her daughter's eye when she brought a book home from school, and wanted to grant her the pleasure of owning her own book.

"Well, we'll see on Christmas morning won't we now," Margaret told her daughter as a glimmer of hope spread across her little girl's pale face. "Right now, we'd better get back before the babies do Mrs Regans in." They both smiled. These outings were indeed a delight for mother and daughter.

As the chilly winds of Autumn whipped up the coal dust on the streets, Margaret knew she was pregnant again. She kept the news to herself. She had never suffered morning sickness and she'd put on so much weight over the past few years that no one would notice. Thomas didn't need the extra pressure as there had been trouble at the mine and all the men were concerned about safety. Death and serious injury were well known in the mining community as men and boys fell down mine shafts or were crushed to their death by tons of falling rock, leaving grieving widows and mothers to rely on the generosity of family and friends for their very livelihood. Margaret heard her husband and sons talking about safety issues and the list of grievances they had taken to the mine owners, but she left it for them to sort out. Her job was to try not to worry about them and make their lives as happy as possible.

***

Festivals were held in Muirkirk in February and December each year and they were always cause for great enjoyment. Dances and festivals were the only chance the young men and women got to meet up socially. The women aired and pressed their Sunday best, added new ribbons to their bonnets, darned socks and polished shoes. The festivals were a family affair and an opportunity to have some fun. George, Thomas and William were looking forward to the December festival as they were all of the age where they were looking to find a mate and there were plenty of girls from surrounding villages, some who would happily give their affections to any lad who showed an interest, and others who were more selective about choosing a future husband. George was hoping that Mary Hamilton would be at the festival and he was going to ask her to dance. Thomas, the only person in whom George had confided his admiration for Mary, enjoyed having fun at his brother's expense.

"Do ye think there'll be anyone special at the festival this year Geordy," he asked at the dinner table one Sunday. Thomas and Margaret looked up from their plates as their son George squirmed in his seat. "Maybe a certain lass that you'll ask for a dance," Thomas continued.

"What's this then Geordy," his father enquired. "Do ye have a lass?"

"No, faither – well – no, faither, it's just I've m' een on a girl but I don't think she knows I'm alive." As Geordy blushed beetroot red, his parents gave each other a sideward glance and got back to their dinner, while Rab and Davey joined in a chorus of "Geordy's got a lassie! Geordy's got a lassie!".

The day of the festival arrived and Thomas had borrowed a horse and cart to take his family into the village. In all their finery, they set off, waving to neighbours who would meet them there.

A ceilidh band was playing when they got to the village green, and tables were laden with pies and cakes. Off in the corner, the men were gathered around with tankards of ale and whisky, laughing and talking. The McMurdo men went off to join them, while Margaret, Lizzie, the children and the babies joined a group of women to catch up on the local news. As the cool of the evening drew in, George saw her. Mary Hamilton was wearing a dark blue bonnet and a blue dress on her slender frame. Her nut brown hair was worn loose in curls and her pale, luminous skin was free of any powder or lipstick. She carried a small, soft cloth blue bag and a book in her gloved hands. She looked plain and serious and was accompanied by her mother who looked even more serious. The Hamilton's were born locally but somehow they didn't seem to fit in.

With his inhibitions lubricated by a few ales, George thought 'it's now or never. I've got to make my move'. He straightened his cap and jacket, threw back his broad shoulders and marched across the village green to where Mary was standing. As he removed his cloth cap, he gave a little bow and introduced himself.

"How do ye do Mary, my name is George McMurdo," he said awkwardly. Turning to Mrs Hamilton, he again slightly bowed. "Mrs Hamilton," he began. "Could I take yer daughter for a spin around the floor?."

Mrs Hamilton's bushy eyebrows arched from under her black bonnet. "A spin, Mr McMurdo," she spat. "A spin!". George felt himself going red again.

"Begging yer pardon, may I ask Mary to dance?"

Mary looked at her mother eagerly and George was heartened.

"You may Mr McMurdo, but mind I'll be right here watching," she said stiffly as she eyed him up and down.

"Thank you mother," Mary said as she handed her the book she'd been carrying.

George noticed that Mary and her mother didn't speak the way most people in the area did. While George called his parents 'mither' and 'faither' Mary and Mrs Hamilton used the more formal 'mother' and 'father' – a sort of 'cultured' Scottish accent that was different from the way people spoke in the miners' rows. Mrs Hamilton had pretensions, he thought, but he made a conscious effort to try to impress Mary with his carefully worded conversation.

George lead her by the hand to the dance floor. He cautiously slid his other hand around her tiny waist and clasped her right hand tightly in his as they took their first tentative steps in a waltz.

"How did you know my name?," Mary asked.

"Oh, I've seen ye in the village and I asked around," George said shyly. "I hope ye don't mind but I had to talk to ye," he said more boldly. "I've admired you from afar for some time," and before the words were out of his mouth he wished he hadn't said them. As Mary surveyed George's handsome face she liked the way his sandy hair was brushed back from his forehead and his blue eyes sparkled when he spoke.

"You're a good dancer George McMurdo," she said and George felt his confidence growing.

"Will ye come out with me some time Mary?," he asked.

"I'm out with you now," she replied. He twirled her around the floor as the tempo of the music fastened with the beat of his heart.

Margaret had been watching her son on the dance floor, and throwing an occasional side glance at Mary's mother. George and his much-loved Mary Hamilton danced every dance together at the festival and talked for hours, and by the time it was over they were both in love. They arranged to meet for a walk the following week. Brimming with new-found confidence, George walked Mary back to her mother who was standing with pursed lips and the ever-arched eyebrows.

"I've returned yer daughter safely, Mrs Hamilton. I should like to call on Mary next week and take her walking."

"What work do you do Mr McMurdo?," came the stern reply.

"I work in the Linkeyburn coal mine with my father and two brothers," George said trying ever so carefully to speak in a way that was acceptable to Mrs Hamilton.

"A coal mine, is it?" she said distastefully. "I have plans for Mary that don't include a coal mine."

George's face dropped and Mary, used to her mother's cold manner, decided to rescue him. "What's wrong with working in a coal mine, mother, it's good honest work. Besides," she paused, "father is a stone quarrier."

Mrs Hamilton's eyes grew wide. "He'll not always be a stone quarrier, my girl. We'll be back on the farm one day soon," she said defiantly. The Hamilton's life on a farm had come to an end when crops failed and rent could not be paid. William Hamilton moved his family and took work in the stone quarries. Ignoring her mother, Mary turned to George.

"I would be most pleased to step out with you George. I'll see you next week." Leaving George in a whirl, she took her mother by the arm, turned on her heel and they walked off together, with Mary throwing a cheeky wink across her shoulder at George. His brother Thomas had been leaning against a tree nearby, arms folded across his chest. He walked over to George and nudged him in the ribs with his elbow.

"Ooh," he laughed, "ye'll no' get away with anythin' with that one."

"Aye," George replied, now lapsing into his familiar way of speaking, still staring into the distance to catch the last glimpse of Mary, "she's braw – and she'll be Mrs George McMurdo by this time next year."

"Come on, I'll buy you a dram," Thomas said as he threw an arm around his brother's shoulders and walked towards the other men.

"Not a word, mind," George said. "I want to speak with faither and mither first." Thomas nodded his head in agreement.

Their mother Margaret had been standing nearby and smiled to herself. Here she was, pregnant with her 11th child, and her first-born was talking about marriage. She quickly wiped a soft tear from her eye, then rounded up the children. Her husband Thomas was now in full flight with the other men, singing and dancing a jig around a keg of ale.

"Time for hame, Tommy," she said.

"Time for hame, Tommy," the men around him sang.

"Oh Maggie, just one more," he slurred. Then one by one the women came to their men in a bid to get them home. Margaret motioned the children towards the cart and waited for her husband to finish his drinking. Thomas drained his tankard and slammed it down on the table. "Time for hame lads," he said. As he brushed past one of his neighbours, Anne Sloan, she caught him by the coat tails and pulled him back.

"For God's sake leave that poor woman alone, Tam," she said angrily. "She cannae take much more."

"What are ye talkin' about Annie, I love my Maggie," Thomas said.

"Aye, you love her just a bit too much."

Thomas looked bewildered. "And that's a crime is it, to love yer woman too much?"

"No," said Anne, "but 11 children Tam. That's a lot for any woman and she's no gettin' any younger."

Thomas looked at Anne with the same bewildered look.

"Oh, yer hopeless," Anne said. "She's pregnant again, man. Anyone can see that," and away she walked in disgust. Thomas walked slowly towards the cart, and climbed up beside his wife who was nursing babies Mary and Margaret.

"Come, lass, we'll get ye hame and I'll make ye a nice cup o' tea," Thomas said. Margaret looked at him through sleepy eyes and they shared a loving moment between husband and wife. She snuggled into his shoulder and they drove home in silence. She no longer had to carry her secret – just her growing child and the burden of caring for an ever-expanding family.

The lead up to Christmas was always an exciting time in the McMurdo household. While Hogmanay, or the start of a new year, was a more important festival all over the country and was celebrated by most people in Scotland, Margaret felt that the children needed something to look forward to, even if some sections of the Presbyterian Church of Scotland still took a hard line and felt that 'Christ's Mass' was too Catholic and therefore not worthy of celebration. Saying Mass had been banned in Scotland since the time of political leader Oliver Cromwell who believed that frivolity had no place in the lives of those who wished to make it to heaven. While Margaret was a God-fearing woman and a regular churchgoer she couldn't see the harm in having one day of the year when the focus could be on the children. Perhaps it was a romantic notion. She had been given a copy of Charles Dickens' novel *A Christmas Carol* not long after it was published in 1843 and the story of a hard-working man who could scarcely feed his family, and the message of helping the poor, had resonated with her. She read a chapter each night in the early years of her marriage, when the weans were asleep. It was her escape and the only book she had ever been given, so she treasured it and read it to her own children when they were small. They were not well off by any means, but it was the spirit of Christmas that Margaret embraced – a time of giving to those less fortunate and of giving thanks for what they had. Since Queen Victoria's husband Prince Albert had introduced the idea of bringing a Christmas tree into Windsor Castle (as he had done as a child in his native

Germany) in the 1840s, Christmas festivities were gaining popularity across Britain, despite the church's opposition. Not that Margaret and Thomas were that enamoured with English royalty, but they kept up with the news.

Almost everyone in the miners' row shared Margaret's views, and no matter how poor, they found a way to celebrate the festive season with food and gifts. Those among them who could barely keep body and soul together found food and gifts on their doorstep on Christmas morning. The women all made one extra item of knitted or crocheted clothing and gathered together what food they could from each household to make up hampers for those whose budgets did not stretch to Christmas treats or who were not so good at handling domestic affairs. Margaret had spent every night for the past month, after the children had gone to bed, sitting in front of the fire with her knitting needles and crochet hook making socks, gloves and scarves to put in her children's Christmas stockings and she'd made some doilies to go into the charity hampers - 'something pretty for their homes', she thought. No one was well off on the miners' row, but people were in and out of each other's houses a lot and she'd seen how some were living without even the bare necessities. Christmas, she felt, was the time to show some Christian charity and she was happy to help out her neighbours in any way that she could.

On Christmas Eve, the stockings were hung from the mantle place for James, John, Lizzie, Rab, Davey, Mary and wee Margaret. The older boys George and Thomas would receive new tobacco pouches and tobacco and William, now 17, would get his very own razor, aptly named a 'cut throat' because of its straight sharp blade that folded into the handle.

On Christmas morning, the younger children rushed to their stockings. As well as a new pair of socks, gloves and scarf for each of them, knitted by their mother, James got some new pencils and a book to write in, John got new marbles, Rab got a wooden train and Davey a wooden boat. Lizzie closed her eyes and offered up a silent prayer as she plunged her hand into her stocking. And there, like the answer to her prayer, was the beautifully illustrated book she had seen in the shop window.

She wanted to sit in a quiet corner and start reading straight away, but there was no quiet corner and she had work to do, so instead she busied herself with helping her baby sisters reach into their stockings and pull out a soft rag doll each. While the children cluttered the floor playing with their presents, Thomas reached on top of the dresser in the kitchen and handed Margaret a small, dark green box, tied with a thin red bow. The children all stopped playing to watch her unwrap the mysterious box. She carefully undid the ribbon and placed it on the table for later use. She gasped as she opened the box and took out a silver thistle brooch. Thomas looked on with delight.

"Oh, Tommy, it's beautiful," she said.

"So are you lass," Thomas said. "I saved all – well most – of my drinkin' money for a month to get it fer ye."

Margaret hugged her husband in a rare display of affection that made the children feel safe and secure.

"Tommy," Margaret said. "I've somethin' fer ye," and she reached behind the plates on the dresser and pulled out a brown leather pouch and handed it to Thomas. He opened it to find a new clay pipe with a long brown stem. Some of the children gasped.

"It's beautiful Maggie, but how…," she cut him short before he could finish the sentence.

"I seem to have been knitting faster this year and I had some extra things so I sold them to a shop in Muirkirk," she said excitedly. They all laughed, for the older children knew by now that she worked 'faster' when the baby moved inside her as somehow spurring her on to build a secure nest for the new life.

"I love it and I'll tak m' first sook after Christmas dinner." In the mining villages, and in many parts of Scotland, the midday meal was referred to as dinner and the evening meal was tea or supper. Most of the men smoked a pipe as they found it relaxing. It was a pleasant pastime.

Their son George had been keeping company with Mary Hamilton and as well as Thomas, Margaret and their 10 children, William and Jane Hamilton and their daughter Mary had been invited to Christmas dinner. As soon as the family returned from church, the presents were cleared away and preparations for the much looked-forward to dinner were begun.

George had gone to collect the Hamiltons in a borrowed horse and cart, Thomas carried coal from the coal shed, his father stoked the fire to keep a good flame and William, James and John entertained Rab and Davey and the baby girls, while Lizzie, as always, was by her mother's side peeling tatties and neeps. Her mother had taken the red ribbon from her Christmas box and tied it in Lizzie's long, blonde hair and she felt extra festive.

As the family gaily chattered, the door opened and in walked Mr and Mrs Hamilton and Mary. None had been formally introduced and the room went quiet. George, growing in confidence as a man, took the lead.

"Mr and Mrs Hamilton and Mary, may I present my parents Margaret and Thomas McMurdo," and with that Margaret wiped her hands on her flour-covered apron and walked towards Jane Hamilton, hand extended. Mrs Hamilton graciously took Margaret's hand and smiled as she cast a cursory look around the room. "Mr Hamilton, welcome," Margaret said as she moved on to William Hamilton and shook his hand. Then Thomas did the same and started to introduce the children.

"You certainly have a…," Mrs Hamilton paused and chose her words carefully, "…lot of healthy children," she continued. Sensing her indignation, Margaret's hackles were up.

"And another one on the way!," she said proudly. "My Thomas is some man, is he no'?," she said to Mrs Hamilton whose pursed lips parted in shock and her husband laughed the laugh of a man who had been waiting all his life to meet his wife's match. Margaret then moved on to Mary, the girl she felt would be her first daughter-in-law. "And you're Mary," she said gently hugging the girl. "Welcome to our home Mary. Geordy has told us all about ye and we've been longin' to meet ye."

"Thank you Mrs McMurdo," Mary said confidently as she shot a sideward glance at her mother. "You have a lovely home full of warmth and cheer and I'm so glad to be here." With the ice broken, George ushered Mr and Mrs Hamilton to the two good chairs in front of the fire and Mrs Hamilton's demeanour seemed to thaw as her bones warmed after being out in the snow. Lizzie put down the bowl that she had been washing potatoes in and walked over to Mary Hamilton who was standing with her hands behind her back.

"Our Geordy said ye work on a farm, Mary. What's it like to work on a farm?"

"Well now Lizzie, there are lots of pigs and sheep and cows – and they smell a bit."

"Ooh," said the boys who were now quite interested in Mary.

"I milk the cows and feed the pigs and gather in the rye."

"Ooh it sounds fascinatin'," Lizzie said. 'Fascinating' was a word she had read in a book at school and she had been longing to use it in conversation.

"And," said Mary Hamilton producing a large cloth bag from behind her back, "on the farm they have blueberries and blackcurrants and lots of other fruit growing, and what do you suppose I have in here?" she asked.

"A wee pig," piped up Davey as he moved towards the bag to see.

"No," Mary laughed. "I picked raspberries in the summer and I made some jam – and there's plenty for everyone to have a jeely piece," she said taking three large glass jars of jam from the bag. The children squealed with delight as freshly-made raspberry jam was a treat. "And," Mary continued. "After your dinner, I've a bag of sweeties for you to share," and she held the brown paper bag high over her head as the children clamoured and tried to reach them. Margaret looked on approvingly and caught Mary's eye across the table. The women smiled at each other and they knew at once that they would be firm friends. Ten-year-old John sidled up to his brother Geordy.

"This Mary's awright Geordy. I think we like her," he said. George could relax. His Mary had been welcomed as one of the family and he had the approval of his mother. The two most important women in his life liked each other and even if Mrs Hamilton proved to be a problem for him, he was sure that between his wife-to-be Mary and his mother Margaret, there was no problem they couldn't solve.

Chapter 3 (1863)

FOR BETTER OR WORSE

He came earlier than expected and could have done with another month in his mother's womb, but Margaret could no longer hold him inside her. The constant lifting of heavy water buckets and washing baskets had seen her take to her bed many times in the past two months with strains and aches and pains. Now her time had come again. At noon on March 6, 1863 Andrew Stevenson McMurdo was born at just six pounds, but healthy. Her neighbour Mrs Regans was again in attendance and cast a wicked look at Thomas as her work was done and she closed the door and went back to her own family. Newspaper was placed inside the cradle for extra warmth for his tiny body, and little Andrew slept peacefully beside his exhausted mother. Margaret now had a tiny baby who would need extra care, one year old Margaret, two year old Mary, four year old Davey and six year old Rab who needed her attention, while the older children helped where they could, but the responsibility of keeping them all clean and fed was hers alone. Ten days after he was born, when they were both a little stronger, Andrew Stevenson McMurdo was christened in the Church of Scotland, Muirkirk where his ten brothers and sisters had also been christened.

Two weeks before his baby brother had been born, George, now 23, had asked William Hamilton for his daughter's hand in marriage. William could see that George was a hard-working man and that he loved Mary, and that, as far as William was concerned, was all he could hope for in a son-in-law. Despite some opposition from his wife, and Mary's tender age of 18, William Hamilton gave his blessing to the young couple.

"Eleven children," Mrs Hamilton had said to Mary when she realised that her daughter was serious about the young coal miner. "Eleven children – is that how you see yourself in the future, Mary. Married to a dirty coal miner, barely scraping by in a two-room house?"

Mary had never been afraid to speak up to her mother. In fact, her forthrightness was one of the qualities George most admired about her.

"If God sends me eleven children then I will love them and their father with all my heart," she answered. "Did you not see the love in that house on Christmas Day? That's what I want mother. I'll be a coal miner's wife and be proud of it."

"Well, don't say I didn't warn you Mary," said her mother, stoney-faced. "You've had more learning than some of the lasses around here, and now you're going to waste it."

"How can learning be wasted mother?," she asked. "I appreciate everything you've done for me mother, but I have to make my own life, just as you have done. I'll be happy, I promise you," she said softening her voice and taking her mother's hand. "You'll see."

The Banns of Marriage were announced in the church for three Sundays prior to the wedding, as was required by Church law to prevent people from marrying in haste. Three months after his baby brother had been christened, in the same church George McMurdo, 23, eldest son of Thomas and Margaret McMurdo, married 18-year-old Mary Percy Hamilton, daughter of William and Jane Percy Hamilton, on June 15, 1863. The young couple entered marriage full of hope and love and vowed to support each other no matter what came their way. So full of youth and vitality, they had no way of knowing the sadness that lay before them.

Chapter 4 (1865)

A CHANGE IN THE AIR

In the Winter of 1865, Margaret felt unwell. She had stopped menstruating and was feeling nauseous.

'Oh no, not again. Please God, not again', she silently prayed. She was now 45 years old and feeling every one of her years. She sat at the table in her kitchen clutching a steaming cup of tea as baby Andrew slept and Mary and Margaret played at her feet. Her eldest son George and his new wife Mary had been married almost two years and Mary was about to give birth to their first child.

'I'll be a new mother and a grandmother at the same time', she thought. She gazed into the fire, lost in thought. Her mind went back to that cold, late-Autumn day on November 23, 1838 when she and Thomas were married by Rev Mr Symington in the church at Muirkirk. Her own father Thomas Stevenson had been a coal miner and she'd seen the work her mother Elizabeth had to do – the coal dust covered clothes to wash and repair, the preparation of meals at all hours of the day, the worry on her mother's face every time her father went out the door to the mine. Yet, she had gladly married a coal miner in the full knowledge of what life would be like for her. She and Thomas had a great love for each other. Thomas was amorous and playful and made her feel like the most loved woman in the world. His grandparents had been farmers in Durisdeer, Dumfriesshire but the coal mines offered more secure work and his father had left the family farm to dig coal, and Thomas followed in his footsteps. Like her daughter-in-law Mary, Margaret had been young when she married Thomas who was around the same age as their son George when he married. In fact Margaret was just 16 years of age when she married but they were in love and she was headstrong and wanted to get out and start life away from her parents. Was it history repeating itself? Young Mary would soon learn the trials and tribulations of being a miner's wife and busy mother, but Margaret would be there to help her. She wanted to help Mary prepare for the birth of her first child but the heartache she felt at being pregnant again herself weighed her down and took the joy out of becoming a grandmother for the first time.

As she drained the last drop of tea from her cup, young Andrew stirred and cried. She checked that the wee girls were still playing happily and walked into the bedroom to pick him up from the box bed.

"And I thought you might be the last," she said to the now-soothed toddler as she held him up before her. "Will we ever have a kitchen free of nappies, young Andrew?," she asked her youngest son as he smiled lovingly at her. "Och, come on we'll get ye changed," she said and took off his wet nappy and placed in a pail ready for washing.

The nausea continued for a few weeks and she reckoned that she must be about five months along. But she hadn't felt the quickening and her belly was still soft. She had counted herself lucky that with 11 pregnancies she had given birth to them all without miscarriage. Could this baby be dead inside her and that's why it's not moving, she wondered. She hadn't confided in Thomas about this pregnancy, and she was worried. On a cold Winter's day with snow ankle deep, Margaret kept Lizzie home from school to look after the weans, and walked the two miles into Muirkirk to see a doctor. She had never had a doctor to any of her births and only when someone was very sick or dying was a doctor called. Paying for a doctor to call was seen as an extravagance that few could afford. But she was worried. If this baby was dead inside her, it would have to come out. She fearfully approached the doctor's waiting room, frozen from the long walk, and sat by the fire, nervously wringing her hands, until her name was called.

The doctor's office smelled of leather chairs and antiseptic, but he looked kindly enough under his shock of thick, grey hair and enormous grey moustache that curled slightly at each end. She explained her situation to the doctor and he listened in awe at how she had given birth to eleven children, all of whom had survived.

"Well, you have certainly done a grand job, Mrs McMurdo," said Dr McHale in his cultured Scottish voice. "And if as you say this child has no life in it, we need to know. Could you step behind that screen and take your clothes off and lie down on the table."

Margaret was terrified. The only person who had seen her naked 'down there' was Mrs Regans and a previous neighbour who had helped her deliver her children. Even Thomas had not seen her fully naked as she ensured the room was always dark when they went to bed. Now a strange man would not only see her, but touch her. She did as she was asked and lay on the bed with her knees together and a sheet over her. The doctor pulled back the screen and, uncovering her, began by pressing on her stomach. As gently as he could, he performed an internal examination as Margaret froze in fear. "Get dressed now Mrs McMurdo," he said, washed his hands and returned to sit at the chair behind the desk. Margaret hastily put her clothes back on and, eyes fixed on the ground, walked back to the chair opposite his desk and sat down. Dr McHale leaned across his desk and spoke softly.

"The good news," the doctor began, "is that we won't have to do a procedure."

Margaret sighed with relief. "Then the baby's all right?," she enquired.

"Ah, well that may be the bad news. There is no baby. Sometimes the signs of pregnancy can be confused in a woman your age. It's a bit early, but I believe you are going through the change."

"No baby – are you sure?," she asked, visibly shaken.

"I'm afraid so," the doctor replied. "I'm very sorry."

"Oh, no need to be sorry doctor, for I'm no' upset. Ye see, after eleven children I had hoped Andrew would be the last. Oh no, I'm no' upset."

"Excellent," said the doctor sitting back in his chair with a sigh of relief. "Now have you discussed the change with your own mother?"

Margaret shook her head.

"Right, then you might feel some nausea from time to time, you might get a bit agitated and hot also, and your monthly bleeding will stop permanently, eventually. You will also no longer be able to have children," he said gently. No more bloodied rags to wash out and use over and over again, and no more trying to hide them from the menfolk to save embarrassment for everyone, she thought to herself.

"I'm the mother of eleven children and about to become a grandmother for the first time, doctor. I've never been happier. I cannae wait to tell Tommy," she said excitedly. "My body's my own, at last," she blurted out before she realised what she had said.

She left the doctor's office feeling as light as a feather. Even the cold wind and rain couldn't dampen her mood. Tonight she would kiss each of her children and give thanks to God for every one of them – and offer up a prayer of thanks that at last, after 25 years of being pregnant, her child- bearing years were behind her. She could now look forward to being a grandmother.

Chapter 5 (1865)

MARY MAKES A NEST

After their marriage in June 1863, George and Mary Hamilton McMurdo had taken a house in a miners' row at Smallburn. George was working in the colliery there and, while it was still close in proximity to both the McMurdos and the Hamiltons, it was far enough away for George and Mary to have some privacy. Mary, following the advice of her mother, spent most of the first few weeks of her marriage furnishing the two-roomed dwelling. George wasn't keen to clutter up the space as he revelled in just two people sharing the house, but Mary's mother was insistent that she should have the best that George could afford, which often meant more than he could afford. While Mary wanted to furnish their home to be comfortable for them both, and relishing the new relationship she was developing with her mother, she was sensible enough to know when to say no.

"But you'll need at least four sets of sheets and pillow cases Mary," her mother insisted as she fondled the crisps linens in the haberdashery shop in Muirkirk.

"We can only sleep on one set at a time mother and will buy more when we need them," Mary replied.

"What about this cream and sugar set?," her mother enquired pointing to a delicate white porcelain set with fine red roses. Mary turned over the price tag and moved on.

"I don't think so mother. The queen will not be visiting," she chastised.

"Oh Mary, I only want what's best for you," her mother pleaded.

"I know mother and whatever George can afford is the best for me, so I'll hear no more about it." She was to encounter her mother's well-meaning advice on many occasions, but Mary skilfully deflected her mother's comments and was determined to show her that she was now her own woman.

Mary took great pride in her housekeeping and looked forward to George coming home from his shift at the mine, to show him what she had achieved within the little house that day and to have him try out a new recipe. She had discovered six ways to prepare potatoes! The place was starting to take shape and was as clean as could be. On the mantle place sat the family bible which George's parents Margaret and Thomas had given them for a wedding present. She was looking forward to entering the names of each of her children in the bible, when the time came. They had also given the young couple two sturdy wooden chairs which Thomas had made and they took pride of place in front of the fire. George and Mary shared many happy nights sitting in front of the fire, Mary reading aloud to George from the latest book to take her fancy. How he loved to hear her soft yet commanding voice trip over the words like a song. Her parents had given them a blanket box for storing linen, and two warm woollen blankets. Mary had brought her silver-plated hair brush and mirror set from home as well as her clothes which consisted of a pair of house shoes and a pair of good shoes, two pairs of stockings, two petticoats, two house dresses, one good dress, one good hat, one house cap, two aprons, two sets of under garments, a nightdress and two handkerchiefs. George had put a curtain on a rod in their bedroom and made shelves to store their clothes. He didn't need as much room as Mary, for his worldly possessions consisted of a pair of work boots, two sets of socks, two flannel shirts, two pairs of trousers, two sets of under garments, a work cap, a good shirt and collar, a belt, a tie that he wore to church, a nightshirt, razor strap, mug, comb, two handkerchiefs, braces and a fob watch his father had given him.

The larder that George had made in the kitchen, just like the one his father had made in their house, was well stocked and they were comfortable. George and Mary were very much in love but didn't dare show any display of affection in public. As soon as the sun went down, they clung to each other in their love nest. They would bathe in front of the fire in a tin tub and talk of the future.

Their first wedding anniversary in June 1864 had passed and still it was just the two of them. A whole year alone together was absolute bliss. As the weather started to close in around an Autumn sky in October, Mary felt the first signs that there might be new life within her. While her relationship with her mother had strengthened, it was her mother-in-law Margaret in whom she confided, and Mary's suspicions were confirmed.

"It's highly likely that ye are with child, m' dear," Margaret said. "Rest as much as ye can and take care of yoursel' for in about five months' time, yer life will never be the same again."

Mary couldn't wait to tell George and she ran into his arms as soon as he walked in the door.

"I hope you've enjoyed our time alone together, and the peace," she began, "for it's all about to end." George looked at her quizzically and she couldn't bear to keep him in suspense. "We're about to become three – you'll be a father George McMurdo," she said.

George sat his young wife gently down in her chair by the fire, and held both her hands. He gazed into her eyes then pulled her close to him. "A wean," he said. "I can hardly wait."

Chapter 6 (1865-1870)

HATCHES AND DESPATCHES

George paced up and down outside his house in the cold, dark street as his mother Margaret and mother-in-law Jane attended to Mary. They had been with her throughout the night as she laboured with the birth of her first child. George had sat holding her hand for the first few hours, feeling useless as his young wife cried out in pain during the 'crying' as it was locally known.

"Go and make some tea, George," his mother had said at about five o'clock. He dutifully went into the kitchen, made the tea and placed the cups and teapot on a tray on the kitchen table. "Why don't ye go outside, son," his mother urged. "There's nothing ye can do here and she's in good hands."

And so he found himself pacing up and down as some of his neighbours set off for the day shift at the mines. Each shouted out as they passed George, many of them experienced fathers encouraging him and telling him that it would all be over soon. And it was. Thomas McMurdo, named after his paternal grandfather, was born at 7.15am on May 13, 1865 in the little miner's house at Smallburn, Muirkirk. As soon as he was allowed by his mother-in-law to enter his home, George rushed to Mary and sat on the bed beside her as she cradled their new-born son. He took the child in his arms and kissed Mary softly on the lips. She smiled.

"Are you pleased George that you have a son?," she asked her husband.

"Aye, I'm pleased lass," and he stroked the child's forehead as Mary closed her eyes in grateful sleep.

Ten days later, on a bright Sunday morning, the McMurdo and Hamilton families, and some friends and neighbours gathered at the Church of Scotland in Muirkirk, for the baptism of Thomas McMurdo, lawful son of George McMurdo and Mary Hamilton McMurdo. Mary had knitted a full set of bonnet, booties, vest and coat from the finest white wool she could afford. She hoped that each of her children would wear the same christening outfit. The baby's grandfather was proud of his namesake and first grandchild from his oldest son. As they gathered in George and Mary's home after the service, Grandfather Thomas was the first to propose a toast and wet the baby's head. Calling for 'a wee bit of shush' and holding a dram of whisky high in the air, he began: "To George and Mary and wee Thomas. May life be full of happiness and health – and may they have many more."

"Hoorah," the shout went up from the assembled crowd and they ate and drank for the next few hours. Family friends practised the custom of hanselling the baby by giving him a coin to hold in his hand. This ritual was meant to bring luck and establish how good the child would be with finances in the future. If the baby held on to the coin he would do well, whereas if he dropped the coin instantly he would always be short of money. Baby Thomas held each coin momentarily then dropped it, so no one could be sure of the outcome of the exercise, but everyone had a good time and then walked or staggered back to their own homes. Christenings and weddings were always such joyous occasions among the miners and their families.

***

Two years later in 1867, George and Mary were blessed with a daughter who they named Jane Percy McMurdo, much to the delight of Mrs Hamilton whose maiden name had been Jane Percy. Dressed in the christening clothes that her mother had lovingly made and her older brother had worn, baby Jane was christened in the church at Muirkirk. She was a pretty baby with lots of brown hair, and George and Mary enjoyed the noise that a toddler and a baby brought to their home. Mary's days became busier but she handled the extra work easily and took great pleasure in putting food on the table and keeping her children clean and happy. She would dress little Thomas and baby Jane in their best clothes and proudly push the baby carriage down the street as she visited neighbours. Life was good.

***

The cycle of life continued and while the McMurdo family celebrated the birth of wee Jane, her grandparents Thomas and Margaret received news that Thomas's mother Mary Thomson McMurdo had taken ill. She and her husband George lived at Dalmellington. George had spent his working life in the pits. They were aged and worn out after raising their family in miners' rows and getting by as best they could.

"Your mither's not long for this world, Tommy," Margaret said as she stood in the kitchen of their home with their youngest child Andrew, now 4, by her side. "We've just been to visit her and she's taken to her bed. And yer faither's very frail."

Thomas sat down heavily at a chair by the kitchen table, his hands clenched tightly together in front of him.

"I should do more for them," he said quietly. "What can I do?"

"Well ye won't be doin' any lifting wi' your back," Margaret said. "I'll speak to George and Thomas to take turns to help with carrying in the coal and the heavy lifting, and James, John and Lizzie can take Rab and Davey to visit and help with the cooking and cleaning."

"But ye know how proud they are," Thomas began, "they'll no' take help from anyone."

"Well, the time has come when they need help and they'll take it," Margaret said firmly.

And so it was settled. Margaret set up a roster of her own children to visit their grandparents and to cook, wash and clean for them. The old man and woman were grateful and loved to see the children. They had raised a family of eight children – five boys and three girls - Thomas being the eldest son. Their eldest child Margaret had borne a daughter to coal mine owner

John Ferguson but later married James Baird in 1856, and the other girls Marion and Sarah were busy with their own families, so it was up to Thomas and his brothers William and George to look after their parents. Thomas's mother, Mary Thomson McMurdo, lived to age 79 and passed away on July 28, 1869 from inflammation, at Dalmellington. Her husband George was lost without her and while the children kept up their roster of visits and care, he was lonely – and proud. One day, two years after his Mary had died, George was carrying a basket of coal in to his fireplace when he tripped on the front stoop and hit his head. He lay there unconscious until his grandson Thomas arrived for his turn to fetch and carry for the old man. Thomas got him into bed but there was nothing that could be done. At 80 years of age, his frail body was worn out and he didn't have the strength to go on. On April 26, 1869, old George McMurdo died at Dalmellington.

***

Almost a year after his grandfather's death, George's third child was born on April 17, 1870. George and Mary called their daughter Margaret, after George's mother. The birth of another lovely daughter filled them both with pride. With his growing family, George had looked for greater work opportunities. He moved back to the miner's row at Linkeyburn Square, where he had lived with his parents as a child, to the ground floor of an up and down house at number 81. Upstairs from George and Mary and their three children lived the spinster dressmaker Agnes Kennedy, 42, and her lodger Robert Forsythe, 26, who was an engine fitter in the mines. It was odd for an older woman to have a younger man as her lodger, but times were tough and Agnes needed the money that Mr Forsythe paid for his bed and lodging. Agnes had her privacy in the hole in the wall bedroom, and Mr Forsythe stayed in a box bed in the kitchen. Agnes welcomed the young Mary Hamilton McMurdo to the miners' row and helped her on many occasions with clothes she made for the children.

While it would have been comforting for George to have his parents still living in Linkeyburn Square, Grandfather Thomas and Granny Margaret, as they were now referred to so as not to cause confusion with their namesakes, had recently moved to a better house at 6 Railway Terrace Muirkirk. Still living at home with Grandfather Thomas and Granny Margaret, and working in the mines with their father, were William, 25, James, 21, John, 19 and Rab, 15. Twelve-year-old Davey, Mary, 9, Margaret, 8, and Andrew now 7 were doing well at school. Lizzie, now 17, had taken work as a domestic servant in a private home. She came home on her rare days off and missed her family terribly, but she was old enough to earn money to help the family and she knew that her sisters Margaret and Mary would be a great help to their mother, taking over the chores that she used to do. She missed her father and the many chats that they would have, but she enjoyed earning her own money and could buy her beloved books whenever she wanted.

While some mine owners provided the very basics for their workers, William Baird and Co made sure that schools were built for the children in the miners' rows, and the McMurdo children took full advantage of gaining an education. They were all gainfully employed and that's just the way Granny Margaret liked it. "The Devil makes work for idle hands", she used to tell her children and they knew from an early age that they were expected to contribute to the running of the household, in whatever way they could.

Chapter 7 (1873)

TEA WITH THE QUEEN

Their time at Linkeyburn Square was short and, as was the lot of miners, George and Mary were once again on the move, this time to a little house in Main Street, Muirkirk. Mary was overjoyed that this house had a roughly tiled floor, instead of compacted bare earth, and she set about creating as attractive a home as she could for her growing family. She was glad to be closer to shops, especially as she was again heavy with child.

On February 7, 1873 George and Mary were blessed with their fourth child whom they named Douglas Percy McMurdo. Mrs Hamilton was pleased that the child bore both her maiden name of Percy and the Christian name of her great-uncle. And while offering a stern word when she felt it was needed, and keeping her grandchildren at arm's length, she loved them dearly and was secretly proud of how her daughter Mary had taken to motherhood, though she would never tell her so.

Mrs Hamilton would often invite herself over to Mary's house for afternoon tea and while Mary loved to see her mother, it was time that she could ill afford to spend sitting about gossiping, for Mrs Hamilton loved to gossip. With four children and a husband to cook and clean for, Mary's days were filled with laborious tasks and she tumbled into bed most nights exhausted.

On one of her visits on a warm September afternoon, Mrs Hamilton sat at the kitchen table in Mary and George's tidy little home, sipping tea from a china cup and saucer and reading the headlines in the *Ayr Advertiser*, while Mary saw to the children and made preparations for the evening meal.

"Ooh," cried Mrs Hamilton as she put down her tea cup and focused on the newspaper. "Queen Victoria will cruise the Caledonian Canal on her way to Balmoral next week. She'll travel on the paddle steamer *Gondalier* which was built specially for use on the canal," she read aloud to Mary. "Oh Mary," Mrs Hamilton cried excitedly as she placed the newspaper on the table. "I've had the most wonderful idea. Why don't we go to see her?"

Mary looked at her mother with a stoney face, pursed her lips and blew an errant strand of hair off her forehead as she dried her hands on her apron. "I've no time for such frivolity, mother," she said with just a hint of anger on her face. "Besides, I've no wish to see the Queen of England."

"She's the Queen of Scotland too Mary," reminded her mother.

"Don't be saying that when my George is at home, mother. He doesn't care for such talk and well you know it."

"Oh, but Mary, you never get out of this dirty miners' row." She paused for thought and began again quickly. "We could take tea on the riverbank – we could have tea with the Queen – well as she passed by – but nevertheless tea within touching distance of the Queen..."

Mary cut her mother short as she carried on with her fanciful plan.

"I'll not hear another word about it mother. I'm sure Queen Victoria will have enough dedicated followers to welcome her to Scotland – she'll no' miss you or me."

Mrs Hamilton wanted to press the point, but seeing the look on her exasperated daughter's face, thought better of it and returned to drinking her tea. Mary turned from the table to the fireplace to stir the stew and her body began to shake with laughter. She turned back to her mother.

"Tea with the Queen," she laughed. "Oh, mother!"

"I told you to buy those expensive cups and saucers," said Mrs Hamilton as she started to laugh as well. It was a lovely moment between mother and daughter as they became closer with each passing year.

Mary felt truly blessed to have a hard-working, loving husband, four healthy children, wonderful in-laws, a doting father and a relationship with her mother that she had once never imagined. At age 27, she seemed to have it all.

Chapter 8 (1874)

ANOTHER ON THE WAY

By Christmas 1874, Mary knew the tell-tale signs of pregnancy. Their fifth child was on the way and, despite her mother's misgivings before she married George, about being 'burdened' with a large family, Mary was thrilled. The children were all still too young to be of much help around the house and Mary was bone weary at the end of every day. Seven-year-old Jane did what she could to help with her younger sister Margaret, 4, and brother Douglas, nearly 2, while nine-year-old Thomas fetched the wood and water before and after school, but Mary was thin, despite being well advanced with child.

After George left for work at dawn on May 28, 1875 and Thomas and Jane were off to school, Mary gave the younger children their breakfast and began clearing up the dishes. As she scooped up the porridge bowls from the table she felt faint and sat down at the table with her head in her hands. Wee Margaret and Douglas looked at each other and while Douglas kept eating his breakfast, little Margaret had a feeling that her mother was not well.

"Shall I fetch Mrs Campbell, mither," the little girl said to her mother Mary who was now pale and drawn.

"Aye, Margaret, run up the road and tell her that my time is coming."

Little Margaret eyed her mother curiously then leapt from her seat at the table and ran out the door. Within 10 minutes Margaret Campbell (known as Mag) was in Mary's kitchen helping her walk from the table to the bed. It was 9am and the miners' row was busy with women hanging out their washing in the only sunlight they'd seen in a week, and small children bouncing balls against the walls of the houses.

"Oh, it's too early Mag," Mary began as she clutched at her stomach and winced in pain. "I've another three weeks to go."

Mag looked at Mary officiously. "You're well on the way Mary and this child will be born today, nothing surer. I'll set up and send your weans next door to Mrs McConnell."

Mary laboured for another two hours and at 11am George and Mary McMurdo's fifth child Andrew Stevenson McMurdo was born. His middle name was taken from his Granny Margaret Stevenson McMurdo and he bore the same name as his twelve-year-old uncle Andrew.

The baby weighed just 5 pounds 3 ounces but he seemed healthy and began to suckle from his mother's breast immediately. Mary was exhausted and could barely hold the child.

"There, now, we'll let you rest for the day. I'll take care of the baby and the weans and make sure there's something in the pot for George coming home," said Mag tenderly.

George and Mary's first-born child Thomas slept in the box bed in the kitchen, with his toddler brother Douglas, while Jane, 7, shared a bed with Margaret, 4, in their parents' room. Mag set about straightening up the increasingly crowded little house, for she knew that Mary liked things to be just so.

When George returned at 4pm from his day shift at the mine, the children were home from school and Mag was bent over a large pot of stew over the fireplace.

"Hello there Mag," George began. "Where's my Mary?"

"She's in bed wi' a wee man," Mag laughed and threw her hands in the air. George stood momentarily glued to the spot then walked slowly into the bedroom. There, sleeping peacefully in the cradle, was his third son Andrew. They had decided on the name some weeks before. And, Mary, pale and thin against the white sheets, opened her eyes and smiled weakly.

"Are you awright, lass?," George asked as he took Mary's hand in his and sat down on the bed beside her. "I didnae expect to come home to this today."

"Are you pleased, George?," Mary asked her husband who was still covered in the dust from his day in the mine.

"Pleased, lass," he said. "I'm more than pleased. You've done me proud again."

And as Mary drifted back to sleep, George went to the wash-house to wipe away the grime of the day.

Andrew's christening took place a few days later in the family's church in Muirkirk as all the McMurdos and Hamiltons gathered to welcome another member of the family.

After the ceremony George and Mary's little house was full of men smoking pipes, women organising food and children playing and laughing. The sun shone as the last days of Spring gave way to the hope and expectation that Summer always brought.

Chapter 9 (1875)

CHILDREN AND MOTHERS

The Summer of 1875 was wet and dreary. The little house at Main Street Muirkirk was damp and cold, but Mary made it as cheery as she could for her growing family. Her husband George grew weary and she herself felt an ache in her bones, but she was made of stern stuff and soldiered on without complaint. Thomas and Jane were home from school for a week of Summer holidays and Mary was glad of their help in looking after little Margaret and Douglas so that she could give extra care to baby Andrew. He was born prematurely and slightly underweight and despite her efforts he failed to thrive. On the few precious sunny days, Mary put him in his crib in the sun 'to strengthen his bones'. He fussed at her breast and often refused to feed. As well as her usual daily chores of cooking, shopping, cleaning and washing she had the added responsibility of keeping the older children amused in the house when it was too wet for them to go out to play. The children cried and fought from the boredom of being cooped up and the baby screamed relentlessly. Mary felt that she could scream herself and quickly devised a plan to quieten her brood.

"Right, then," she said loudly over the din as she clapped her hands like a frustrated school teacher to get the children's attention. "How about we get a start on the Christmas decorations."

"Christmas, is it nearly Christmas?", five-year-old Margaret asked excitedly.

"No, silly it's months away," said eight-year-old Jane as she slumped down on a chair at the table.

"Oh don't be such a sourpuss Janie," her mother said. "I think this year that you are old enough to show wee Dougie how to make paper chains," she paused, "and Thomas you can help Margaret make a Christmas stocking for baby Andrew."

The children looked mildly interested until Janie spoiled the mood.

"But we've no coloured paper, mither. How are we to make beautiful decorations with no paper?"

Mary thought quickly. She usually bought a few extra sheets of coloured paper to add to the decorations each year but as it was only August, she hadn't yet made the trip to the stationery shop. Desperate times called for desperate measures and she spied her treasured copy of *The Scots Magazine* which her mother had left on her last visit.

She walked quickly over to her chair by the fireplace and snatched up the magazine.

"Well, then this year we'll have extra special decorations. Everyone take some pages and I'll make some glue with flour and water. Thomas and Janie you are in charge of the scissors, mind the weans don't cut themselves, and away you go. Margaret fetch my sewing box and you'll find some material to make Andrew's stocking."

The children busied themselves doing as they were told and reassembled back at the kitchen table, their little hands occupied and their minds focussed on Christmas. Suddenly the household was quiet and Mary turned her attention to the baby. If he hadn't put on some weight in a week or two she would take him to see the doctor.

The children were back at school, Summer drew to a close and the chilly winds of Autumn whipped up the leaves on the trees.

Mrs Hamilton came by for one of her afternoon tea visits. She had brought a butter cake for her and Mary to share, but Mary put her piece aside to give to the children when they got home from school.

"Are you not eating, Mary?," her mother enquired. "You look terrible, girl," she berated as she raised the tea cup to her lips.

"And what's wrong with this wean, crying all the time. Are you not feeding him?"

Mary was worn down and she didn't need her mother's criticism. She would have liked to confide in her, woman to woman, but she still found that very hard to do.

"He's just a tiny one is all," Mary said as she moved to Andrew's crib and lifted him out. "Would you like to hold him, mother?"

"Oh, when I've had my tea – and I'm wearing my best dress Mary as I'm going to visit Reverend Symes and his wife after I leave here. I've been asked on to the church committee, you know. I wouldn't want to arrive with baby spit all over me."

"Of course not," Mary said with a hint of anger in her voice as she cradled the three-month-old baby in her arms. She did her best to keep him warm and dry and fed, but he never seemed satisfied and she wished that she could ask her mother's advice. Instead, she made up her mind to talk to her mother-in-law Margaret. After all, as her mother continued to point out, Margaret was the mother of 11 children. She'd know what to do.

Mary was interrupted in her thoughts as the door opened and George arrived home from his work. His eyes were immediately drawn to his wife and child and he smiled lovingly. Then his face dropped as he became aware of Mrs Hamilton seated at the head of the table taking tea.

"Hello mither Hamilton," he said politely as he hung up his cap on the hook by the door.

"Oh George, look at you tracking dust and dirt all over the place. Hasn't Mary got enough to do with four children and a sick baby to look after?," she asked without bidding him hello.

George ignored her – he'd found this was the best strategy for dealing with her – and walked over to Mary.

"Is he no' well Mary?," he asked as his dusty, black hand landed on the shoulder of her grey house dress.

"Well, he's no better George," she began. "I'm thinking of taking him to see your mother to see what she makes of him."

Before she realised what she had said, Mrs Hamilton was on her feet and gathering up her dark grey shawl and matching bonnet.

"I'll be off then – musn't keep the Reverend and his wife waiting," Mrs Hamilton declared and stood at the door waiting for George to open it for her. George dutifully opened the door, and she walked through with a flourish of her shawl and trotted off down the street. As George closed the door behind him and leaned against the wall, he heard shouting from up the street. Mary, still carrying Andrew, rose from her seat to look out the window – and there was Mrs Hamilton wiping mud from her dress and berating the children who had jumped in a puddle just as she passed by.

"I shouldnae laugh George, but it's the best entertainment I've had all day," Mary giggled, slipping into her husband's way of speaking. Any opportunity to take her mind off her heavy workload and worrying about baby Andrew, was welcome – even if it was at her mother's expense.

George finished cleaning the dust off himself in the back wash-house and picked up his pipe from the mantelpiece. The children were all home and Mary busied herself getting the tea on the table. Andrew began to cry and she looked to George as he lit his pipe and began to settle himself in his chair by the fire.

Her gaze was strong and George knew that look. Despite all their happiness, Mary was still the strong, feisty girl he fell in love with and sometimes her looks could wilt a rose.

Before his backside had hit the chair, George was up and walking to the bedroom, pipe firmly clenched between his teeth.

"I'll be gettin' the baby Mary while you get on with the tea," he said in his attempt at holding some authority in the household and appeasing his wife. He picked up Andrew and took him back to the seat by the fire to enjoy his pipe. Mary smiled to herself and stole a glance at father and child in a tender moment. Few men in the miners' rows would offer to help with the children. How she loved that man.

Chapter 10 (1875)

A FAMILY'S LOSS

Autumn leaves of russet and gold covered the coal-strewn streets outside the miners' row to the delight of the children who played amongst them. The cold wind whistled through their thin clothing and with no shoes on their feet they were glad to get into the house to the warmth of the fire. By mid-October, baby Andrew had developed a cough. Granny Margaret offered advice to Mary when she asked for it, and tried to keep her spirits high, but she was concerned about her grandchild. He constantly had a runny nose and had developed breathing problems. Mary and George put it down to a cold as the older children always caught colds when the weather changed, but there was something else. Mary noticed that his nappies were rarely wet.

For a fortnight the baby's breathing difficulties increased and he had started pulling at his ear and crying in pain. Mary awoke at 1am on the morning of November 4 to the sound of laboured breathing and to find that Andrew had a fever and was listless. Within the hour his condition had worsened and his lips turned blue. George was at work and the other children were all asleep. Mary picked up baby Andrew, wrapped him in a shawl, and ran up the road to Mag Campbell who took one look at the child and called to her husband John. "Fetch the doctor quickly," Mag said to her husband as she walked Mary and the baby back to the McMurdo house where the older children Thomas and Janie were sitting bolt upright in their beds. As John Campbell started to walk quickly towards the doctor's office he saw Dr Robert Stevenson (no relation to Granny Margaret) leaving a nearby residence after sitting with a dying patient. John summoned the doctor to the McMurdo house where Mary and Mag were seated on the bed, with five-month-old Andrew cradled in Mary's arms. He had stopped crying and was limp. As the doctor walked through the door he took one look at the child and stared knowingly into the eyes of Mag Campbell. He took the baby from Mary's arms and examined him, but it was too late. Little Andrew Stevenson McMurdo died of bronchitis at 2.45am on November 4, 1875. The doctor placed his lifeless body into the cradle beside his parents' bed.

"I'm sorry Mrs McMurdo but he's gone," the doctor began. "It was acute bronchitis. It's quite common in premature babies," he said as though that was somehow to bring comfort to the grieving young mother. He continued clinically, "his airways were constricted and dust and smoke exacerbated the condition." He knew that Mary wasn't listening to him and he began writing out the death certificate as Mag Campbell put a comforting arm around Mary who sat quietly in disbelief.

Incredibly, wee Margaret and Dougie had slept through the commotion and stirred from their beds around 6am.

Margaret saw her mother sitting on the bed and wondered why she wasn't in the kitchen preparing the porridge. She leapt out of her box bed and bounded into the bedroom to cuddle her mother and then, as she did every morning, peeped into the cradle to talk to Andrew. Her little hand reached to stroke her baby brother's fingers.

"Ooh," she cooed. "Your wee hands are frozen Andrew," and she pulled his baby blanket up around his neck. Turning to her mother, who still sat incredulously on the bed, she asked "Where's our porridge, mither." Mary looked at her little daughter for a few moments then suddenly realised that life had to go on. She had to somehow function and continue to care for her family without her baby at her breast. She felt numb and knew she had to get up off the bed, but didn't know how to put one foot in front of the other. She gazed at her lifeless child and took a tentative step, but fell to the floor weeping. Her heart was breaking and she needed her husband. She needed him now.

Mag Campbell gently put Mary to bed and removed the cradle and baby Andrew into the kitchen. She moved a slatted, tri-fold wooden screen that was used for some privacy when dressing, in front of the cradle. There was little space in the two-roomed miner's house to disguise such a sad event. The doctor and Mag felt it was best to leave the baby in his cradle and to arrange the funeral as soon as possible. After the doctor left, Mag sent her husband to fetch the child's grannies, Margaret McMurdo and Jane Hamilton, and took wee Margaret and Dougie, and Thomas and Janie next door to her house for their porridge, then summoned another neighbour to sit with the children. Then she returned to the McMurdo house, where Mary sat staring out of the house's only window. For now there was nothing that Mag could say that would ease the pain of the young mother, so she quietly moved behind the screen and set about bathing the baby's tiny body and laying him out in a clean set of clothes. She knew that the two grandmothers would be a big comfort to Mary and would help with arrangements for the funeral.

A baby dying in the miners' row was not uncommon, but it was new for the McMurdo family and the whole row felt their sorrow.

As soon as George reached the surface of the pit after his shift was over, his neighbour John Campbell was heading off to start his shift and had to be the bearer of the sad news. George ran all the way to his home and burst through the door. Mary was by now sitting at the kitchen table with a cup of tea thrust into her hands by Mag, as she stared into space. George looked across at Mag who shook her head as if to say 'she's in a bad way'. He knelt down beside her and took her in his arms and Mary's tears fell on his shoulder. His face, still black with coal dust from the day's work, was cleaned in streaks from his own tears and they held each other tightly. They had been so happy for so long and this was the first real trial in their married life. The grannies, Margaret McMurdo and Jane Hamilton, not known for their kinship towards one another, stood in the corner of the kitchen grabbing at each other's forearms as they steadied themselves. The grief in the room was palpable. Mag edged silently out the door and shook her head sadly as she glanced back over her shoulder. Death was a part of life, she thought, but when it first comes knocking it sucks the life out of everyone around.

"May God give you strength, Mary," she muttered quietly and left the family to get on with their business.

George looked across the room to his mother Margaret who walked to the screen and moved it away slightly. He stood beside the cradle and gently touched his baby son's arm. He looked at Margaret and felt as though his heart would break. He straightened his shoulders, wiped away his tears and headed to the wash-house.

"I'm away to the kirk," he said wiping the last drips of water from his face. "You'll look after Mary for me mither, and take the first sitting with Andrew."

"Aye, I will, George," his mother answered. As was the custom, Margaret lit candles around the cradle, then took a chair and placed it beside the cradle where she sat to keep watch over the child. It was partly a superstition that lingered that a family must 'sit up' with the deceased so that the devil could not claim his soul, but it was more a loving gesture within the family.

As Jane Hamilton pulled the screen back into place to shield Mary from the sight of her dead child, she kept her daughter company until George returned with the mort cloth from the church.

Within the hour he had returned. He spoke gently to Mary: "I've arranged with the reverend for the funeral to take place tomorrow, lass. Now come with me as we place the cloth over our wee lad." Together they placed the small, black velvet mort cloth, which George had hired from the church for a fee of 1s 6d, over the tiny body and stood staring down at him.

Jane Hamilton took the next sitting beside the cradle and when both grandmothers were gone, George gathered Mary and his remaining children – Thomas, Jane, Douglas and Margaret – around the cradle and lead them in a prayer for the repose of Andrew's soul.

He then put the children and Mary to bed and sat up all night beside the cradle.

The next day, the local cabinetmaker arrived with a tiny pine coffin and George placed his infant son into the wooden box. The children were dressed in their Sunday best and all the McMurdos and Hamiltons were waiting outside the house. George picked up his son's coffin, draped in the mort cloth, and carried it out the door feet first as was the custom - we come into the world head first, and leave feet first - as he started the sad procession to his son's final resting place. Family, neighbours and friends joined the march in a show of support for the family and bowed their heads at the gravesite as Mary stood supported by her husband, her face emotionless as she stared into the deep hole where the tiny coffin rested.

No, the death of a baby wasn't uncommon in the miners' row, but the pain of the family was felt by everyone.

Chapter 11 (1875)

LEARNING TO LIVE WITH THE PAIN

S even weeks after baby Andrew's passing it was Christmas Eve. The snow and rain had been falling for two weeks and the dirt roads of the miners' row were covered in slush.

Mary was still suffering depression after the loss of her infant son, but she pushed herself through every day for the sake of George and the children. Everyone around her had been very kind, but she knew that she was expected to pull herself together and get on with it. The hole in her heart, she felt, would never heal. On Christmas Eve, young Janie pulled the box from under the bed that contained all of the Christmas decorations and Christmas stockings. As the children excitedly claimed their own Christmas stocking ready to hang by the fireplace, little Margaret called out "what will we do with Andrew's stocking?". The excited chatter stopped suddenly and all was quiet as everyone looked at Mary. With a lump in her throat she made a decision.

"Andrew is still part of this family and we'll hang his stocking with everyone else's," she said. It seemed like just the right thing to say and the family happily continued on getting ready for Christmas Day.

Despite the overhanging sadness, Christmas Day was like every other year – full of family, food and fun. When the last guest had left, Mary put the children to bed, tidied up and said a silent prayer for her family before sliding into bed with her husband.

Hogmanay was the usual round of drinks at neighbours' houses before everyone gathered in the road outside the houses at midnight to sing *Auld Lang Syne*. It had been a hard year and Mary was glad to say goodbye to it. She looked into the clear night sky and made a wish that 1876 would be a fresh new year with no sadness in it.

Chapter 12 (1876)

LEARNING TO LIVE WITH MORE PAIN

All throughout January and February the snow continued to fall. The little house at Main Street Muirkirk was showing wet patches in the brick work and the children wore both their sets of clothes to bed and cuddled together to keep out the cold. Ten-year-old Thomas and his two-year-old brother Douglas slept in the bed in the kitchen, and eight-year-old Jane and five-year-old Margaret shared the smaller box bed in their parents' room. The privy, which was basically an ash pit, was some distance from the house and shared by four other families so to avoid having to go out in the night in the freezing snow, chamber pots were kept below the beds for calls of nature. It was Jane's job to empty the chamber pots each morning, a job she hated but she never complained.

Mary was most insistent about personal hygiene in the home and regular washing of hands, but some other families in the row didn't always have hygienic practices. Their playground was among the midden heaps and the neighbourhood children were always picking up colds and sores from each other.

"Get it once, you'll no get it again", was the general saying in the row, regardless of the ailment. One of the easiest conditions to spread was gastroenteritis which could be directly related to hands not being washed after visiting the crude ashpits, and this winter it was rife among the children of the row. Wee Margaret had come down with a case of diarrhoea, or the skitters as it was known locally, and her mother Mary had kept her in bed for a week and fed her on broth and bread. In the middle of the night Jane appeared at her mother's bedside and shook her arm gently.

"Mither," she began, "wee Margaret's burnin' up." Mary rose from her bed clad only in her thin nightdress and moved quickly to her daughter's side as she instructed Jane to fetch a candle for light. As she placed a hand on Margaret's forehead she felt the heat radiate from the child's head. Jane moved the candle closer and Mary noticed that Margaret's nose was bleeding. She was listless and sweating.

"Jane," Mary said, "fetch me a cloth and a bowl of water and mind not to wake your father and brothers."

Jane lit another candle for her own use and set about doing as she had been asked. When she returned Mary took the cool cloth and pressed it against Margaret's forehead. "Go back to bed Janie," she whispered. "Get in with your brothers."

Mary sat with her sick child for three hours until the household started to stir for the day. There was no change in Margaret's condition as she lay on the bed, her nightdress drenched in sweat and her dark hair clinging to her head.

"I'm keeping Janie home from school today George," she told her husband. "I'll send her to fetch your mother. I'm going to need help to care for Margaret."

George nodded and touched his little girl gently on the cheek as he headed off to work.

Jane arrived at the door of her grandparents Margaret and Thomas McMurdo and knocked softly. The door opened wide and there stood her grandmother wiping her hands on her apron.

"Well, hello there wee Janie, what are you doing here? Why are ye no' at the school?," her grandmother asked.

"Oh, Granny," she began, "me mither has asked for ye to come – wee Margaret's no' well." The expression on Margaret McMurdo's face changed from a wide grin to a furrowed brow. She gathered up her shawl and bonnet and started out the door. Granny Margaret stopped in her tracks then spun around. "Oh, I must leave a note for yer Grandfaither for when he comes hame from the day shift," she said and hurriedly scribbled a note which she left on the kitchen table. She closed the door behind her and together they trudged through the snow from Railway Terrace to George and Mary's house in Main Street.

They were thankful of the warm fire when they reached the house and Granny Margaret looked sadly at her daughter-in-law Mary as she bent over her sick child. 'Please God', Granny Margaret silently prayed, 'don't put her through any more pain', then, summoning up her cheeriest voice, walked over to the bed.

"How's m' wee Margaret Stevenson McMurdo?," she said to the child. "You've exactly the same name as me ye know, lass. Exactly the same – now isn't that something?," she asked trying to cajole the ailing child who opened her eyes momentarily. "Janie make your mither a cup o' tea and a bowl o' porridge and I'll see to the wean."

Granny Margaret took Mary by the arm and lead her to the table. "On ye go, lass, I'll take over fer a while," she said as she took the chair beside the bed and wiped her grand-daughter's fevered brow.

For three days and three nights Granny Margaret sat with her namesake but still the fever had not broken. Wee Margaret was delirious and calling out to creatures only she could see. Her stomach had become distended and painful to the touch and the diarrhoea had returned.

Mary was sick with worry and her mother-in-law felt it was time for decisive action. "We've got to send fer the doctor Mary," she said calmly. "This fever should have broken by now and I don't like the way her stomach looks."

Pulling up the bed covers around the writhing child, she rose from her seat and gathered up her shawl and bonnet. "I'll go fer him mysel'. Janie look after yer mither and keep the cool cloths up to wee Margaret."

Truth to tell, Granny Margaret was glad to get out of the little house with its smell of sickness and air of despair, and into the crisp white snow. She had a hollow feeling in the pit of her stomach and marched as quickly as her ageing legs would carry her. Within two hours she was sitting in Dr Stevenson's carriage as they drove along the unpaved streets back to Main Street.

Dr Stevenson stooped as he entered the house through the low doorway, and removed his hat. He sat down beside wee Margaret and took out his stethoscope and listened to her heartbeat, opened her mouth and looked inside, and felt around her abdomen. He then produced a thermometer from his bag.

"What's that Doctor?," Mary asked as he placed the thermometer in wee Margaret's mouth.

"This my dear woman is the first practical thermometer for taking a patient's temperature," Dr Stevenson replied. "It was invented about nine years ago by an English physician called Thomas Allbut."

"But what does it do?," Granny Margaret enquired.

"As physicians we have come to realise that a high temperature can tell us a lot about the progress of an illness. If your child has a high temperature then her illness is getting worse," he said bluntly. After five minutes, he took the thermometer from wee Margaret's mouth, shook it down and, looking at Mary who was hovering behind him, he said: "Your child is dehydrated and she has a temperature of 103."

"Is that bad Doctor?," Mary asked. Doctor Stevenson smiled at the child, then turned towards Mary.

"I've treated six cases of enteric fever and typhoid in the past week Mrs McMurdo. I believe wee Margaret has typhoid."

"What does that mean Doctor?," Mary asked as she glanced across at her mother-in-law.

"It means that we need to get her fever down and treat her for the dehydration and diarrhoea. I'd like to see her in the hospital."

Mary picked up her child in her arms while Granny Margaret wrapped a warm blanket around her namesake's tiny body and Mary went with the doctor in his carriage to the hospital. When George returned from work, his mother Margaret stayed with her grandchildren Thomas, Jane and Douglas while George walked the mile to the hospital. The smell of antiseptic filled his nostrils as he entered the big dark building, and it brought back memories of the two weeks he had spent there after the mining accident that saw him off work for a month with broken ribs. A short, stout, officious nurse dressed in a starched white uniform showed him to wee Margaret's bed with orders not to upset her or stay for long. The child looked even paler against the crisp white sheets, as her long dark hair fell across the pillow and her eyes had sunken into her head. He gently touched Mary on her shoulder and spoke to the child.

"Hello there darlin'," George said as he stroked an errant strand of hair from her face. "How are ye feelin'?," but wee Margaret didn't answer – just fluttered her eyelids as her eyes rolled back in her head.

"Don't cry baby," she suddenly said, "don't cry" as she reached out her hand. Mary and George looked at each other.

"She's delirious," said the nurse matter-of-factly. "She's had occasion to call out a few times during the day, but it makes no sense. It's typical of the disease."

Mary began to cry and was comforted in the strong arms of her husband.

"That's all for now," said the nurse, motioning them to the door. "You can come back again tomorrow."

For five days they trudged to the hospital, each day hoping for an improvement, but it never came. Margaret was refusing to eat and had developed a rash on her skin. The diarrhoea gave way to vomiting and the light hurt her eyes.

On April 17, it was wee Margaret's sixth birthday. Early in the morning, her parents bought a patchwork rag doll and wrapped it in blue paper with a white ribbon. Perhaps the gift would cheer up their little girl, they thought. They arrived at the hospital and were greeted by Dr Stevenson. He took them both aside to tell them what he had suspected for days.

"I'm afraid Margaret has developed meningitis," he said grimly. "She has no strength to fight the infection. I think you should sit with her now."

Mary and George walked the long corridor to the darkened room where Margaret had been placed. She no longer called out in delirium or opened her eyes. Her breathing was laboured. Mary sat by the bed, unwrapped the doll and placed it in the crook of wee Margaret's right arm.

"Happy birthday darlin'," she said as the tears rolled down her thin face.

Then suddenly Mary stood up. "I want her home, George," she screamed. "I want her home. This place is so cold. I want her with us," and she dissolved into George's arms as his own chest heaved from the tears that were welling within him. They arranged to have the child transported back to their little house in Main Street, Muirkirk, and within hours of her returning home, on her sixth birthday, wee Margaret Stevenson McMurdo breathed her last breath.

Just five months after the loss of baby Andrew, the little house on Main Street was once again darkened by death and sadness. Wee Margaret's body was cleansed and laid out on the bed in her parents' room. She was dressed in a plain white calico dress, her long dark hair brushed and falling around her head on the pillow. George made the journey once again to the church to hire the mort cloth to cover his little girl. Family and friends filed through the little house to pay their respects to the family, some pausing to quote bible passages over the child's body. Mary sat beside wee Margaret's body for two days and two nights. Neighbours brought extra coal to keep the fire stoked and to keep the dark little house warm through the dead days, as they were known.

Two days after her passing, wee Margaret's father George and her Grandfather Thomas carried her little body in a pine coffin draped with a mort cloth to the Muirkirk Cemetery where she was laid to rest beside her baby brother Andrew. Wee Margaret was buried with her birthday doll, and another piece of her mother's heart.

Chapter 13 (1876)

A MAN'S GOT TO BE A MAN

T he few bright days of Spring were overshadowed by the ever-present sadness in the little house at Main Street. After wee Margaret's funeral, Mary went into a further decline. The deep lines etched on her plain but pleasant face made her look older than her 30 years, and she kept much to herself. Even her husband was kept at arm's length and she made sure that she went to bed long after him, for fear he would take her in his arms and she would start crying and never stop. She scrubbed and scrubbed the house, washing away the damp and moss as though the process would cleanse her of the painful memories of the loss of two children. She seemed to have lost interest in her three remaining children, Thomas, Jane and Douglas, and they were often sent to their grandparents' house, barefoot and hungry.

"So ye've been sent doon to your granny's again have you m' weans," Granny Margaret would say as she opened the door to the three sad little faces. "Well, in ye come and sit yoursels doon and I'll fetch ye some bread and jam."

The children enjoyed their visits to Granny Margaret and Grandfather Thomas. It was a respite from the sadness in their own house, and a mother they could no longer reach emotionally. In their grandparents' house they could play with Uncle Rab, now 20, and Uncle Davey, now 18. Their Aunt Lizzie had fulfilled the prophecy of her mother all those years ago as they stood outside the shop window looking at a picture book. She had indeed married a coal miner, named James Howie, on August 6, 1875 in the family church at Muirkirk. She still had her love of reading and sometimes when her brother George's children would visit their grandparents, Lizzie would be visiting too and she would read to the children. Her niece Jane especially had the same fondness for books as her aunt and they shared a special bond. Their other aunts and uncles had all left home to find work or married and, after caring for 11 children, the house was too quiet. Grandfather Thomas and Granny Margaret loved having the three little bodies in their home to fuss over.

"How's yer mither?," Grandfather Thomas enquired of them all. The older children Thomas and Jane looked at each other, fearful of what to say, while little Dougie continued to enjoy his bread and jam.

"She cleans a lot," young Thomas ventured.

"And she's awfully sad," added Jane.

"Aye," Granny Margaret replied as she walked over to her husband Thomas who was sitting in his usual chair supping on a whisky. "It's been six weeks since we buried wee Margaret you know. I'm worried about Mary. Can ye have a word with our Geordy, Tommy. See if he can bring her out of it."

"Oh, Maggie," Thomas began, "the man's in pain hissel'. And he takes that pain underground every day."

"Well, he's the man of the hoose and his wife needs him," Margaret replied sternly. "Now away ye go and speak to him after his work."

"Aye, I'll take him to The Black Bull," said Thomas.

"Aye, I suppose ye will," Margaret replied sharply, but at least someone was doing something.

Later that night Thomas and his son George returned to the miners' row at Main Street, a wee bit pie-eyed. Drowning their sorrows was the only way men in the rows knew how to cope, but it was a temporary measure. Mary was none too pleased when they arrived on her doorstep in that condition, and chastised them both.

"What do you mean coming into the house at this hour, with drink under your belt," she shouted at them as she started to clean up the mud they had tracked into the house on their boots. "You'll wake the weans and I can't be doin' wi' this."

"That's it Mary, get yer temper up Darlin'," George encouraged. "Tell me I'm a fool," he said as Mary advanced towards him. She began beating on his chest with her fists. "That's it Darlin', let it out," George said as Mary beat him even harder and collapsed in his arms. George picked her up and took her to her bed and held her until she fell asleep. Old Thomas was sitting in the kitchen, tears rolling down his face, when his son George returned.

"It's a hard life ye've been given, son. A hard life." He placed his hand on George's shoulder then turned and left for home.

Chapter 14 (1876)

GETTING ON WITH IT

The Summer of 1876 passed peacefully and some normality returned to the home of George and Mary McMurdo. After making her peace with God for taking her children, Mary started going to church again and the children were being cared for with food and clean clothing, but the affection she showered on them prior to the passing of baby Andrew and wee Margaret was held in reserve as though she was afraid to love them. Children, being children, got about their daily business with Thomas and Jane at school and three-year-old Douglas keeping Mary company during the day.

Summer turned to Autumn then Winter as the cycle of life and death continued on the coalfields and in the miners' rows of western Scotland. As the wind and rain grew colder in the lead up to Christmas 1876, Mary's heart thawed a little and she was back in control of her household. The children noticed the change in her and were able to hug her without fear of rejection. George was also able to get closer to Mary and he noticed that in the past few weeks she had started going to bed at around the same time as him, although he was afraid to do more than kiss her goodnight for he too didn't want to feel her rejection. Although she couldn't be described as happy, Mary was back in the land of the living and functioning as best she could.

For the sake of her children, she went about preparing for Christmas as she did every year. They talked of food and gifts and grandparents visiting and the house was once again full of laughter. When it came time to bring out the Christmas decorations and stockings, Jane pulled out the box from under the bed. Her mother was just starting to feel better, she thought, and she didn't want to upset her again so she hid the two stockings for baby Andrew and wee Margaret under the feather mattress on her box bed, and hung her own stocking next to her brothers Thomas and Douglas on the fireplace mantle.

Grandparents Jane and William Hamilton and Thomas and Margaret McMurdo arrived at the Main Street house for Christmas dinner with gifts for the children, and the little house was brimming with cheer. Between them they had scraped enough money together to buy a turkey which George proudly set about carving. When the plates were full of food and placed before each family member, they bowed their heads to pray. As George finished the blessing, all was quiet until Mary broke the silence. Her head still bowed and her hands clasped before her on the table she spoke.

"I thank God for our children Thomas, Jane and Douglas and ask Him to look after our babies Andrew and Margaret until we can be with them again."

Quietly they all answered "Amen".

"And," Mary continued, "I ask that my family stops worrying about me. I have returned," she said as she looked across the table to her husband who gently wiped a tear from his eye.

"Now, she said, "this turkey's getting cold and it's too expensive to waste," and the general hubbub resumed.

When all the guests had left and the children were tucked up in bed, Mary went to her husband George and held him tightly. They made love for the first time in eight months. Slowly they both felt that their world could be right again.

Chapter 15 (1877)

A NEW MARGARET

On February 7, 1877 as they celebrated Douglas's fourth birthday, Mary knew that another child was on the way. It was early days, but she knew the signs. She kept the news to herself until she could be sure, but in late April as the bright yellow gorse flowers started to bloom on the hills above Muirkirk, she felt the first flutterings of life inside her. When she told George he was overjoyed and she allowed herself to feel happy too.

At the end of Summer, on August 18, 1877 at 11.45pm, Mary gave birth to a daughter whom they also named Margaret Stevenson McMurdo. She was the image of her older sister who had live to just six years age, and it tore at Mary's heart.

"She's not a replacement for our wee Margaret," Mary told her mother-in-law whose name the child was given. "She'll be her own wee person but the name must go on," and Granny Margaret knew what she meant. Tradition had to be followed so that family names could be passed down through the generations.

The new child brought great joy to the family and day by day Mary grew closer to her little daughter. Once again she was diving under nappies hoisted on a rack above the fireplace and enjoyed having the sounds of an infant in the house. In this moment, she was happy.

Chapter 16 (1877)

NO MINES FOR OURS

The Ayrshire mine owners expected their workers to toil for 10 hours a day, sometimes more, in appalling conditions for meagre wages. They wanted the coal that the rich Ayrshire coal fields could yield, and they wanted it at the cheapest cost to sell at the highest price. They grudgingly built miners' rows close to the coal mines for the men and their families and, in the larger mining areas, provided company stores stocking provisions for the average family, which may have seemed liked a benevolent gesture but it really equated to good business. The men earned their wages from the coal owners and spent their wages in the coal owners' stores, at sometimes inflated prices but what were the families to do. With no transportation and most of the miners' rows built beside the collieries and outside villages, the miners and their families were a captive audience who had no alternative than to buy their food and supplies from the mine-owned stores. The houses were built out of the cheapest materials possible as they were always intended by the mine owners to be temporary dwellings to be pulled down once the land was raped of all its coal and they moved on to richer pickings. But the miners' rows were home to the families who lived there, and many in the surrounding communities felt they deserved better living conditions. However, few men would rise up against the mine owners as it meant loss of wages and possibly loss of jobs.

The Blantyre Mines owned by William Dixon were a prime example. Repeated complaints about the working conditions at High Blantyre had been ignored and the miners, so fearful for their safety in the mines, asked for a wage rise to compensate them for long hours toiled in wretched conditions. When the wage rise was refused by Dixon, the men went on strike and were immediately sacked.

Mining conditions were unsafe across all the pits in the area but the impoverished men were all but powerless against the might of the mine owners. They worked shifts across the day and night in cramped, hot conditions, with the ever-present fear of fire, explosion and flooding, to feed their families and keep a roof over their heads.

George McMurdo was a strong and responsible worker and his duties in the mine had been extended to include taking on the role of Fireman under the supervision of a Firemaster. One of the more dangerous elements of coal mining was the highly explosive gas known as firedamp which was easily ignited by flame, friction or electrical energy. Methane or marsh gas was often found in the coal mines and sometimes large volumes of it would be broken into during the mine workings, resulting in what was known as blowers. It was the responsibility of George, and other Firemen, to check the pits for the build up of firedamp and other gases such as carbon monoxide or afterdamp as it was known, which could be suffocating to all those down below. Each day George would carry out his checks before the men were allowed to descend into the mines, and many a day he would have to organise for the burning off in small pockets, or arranging for ventilation forced by furnaces and steam, to remove the gases to make it safe for the men to work. He enjoyed the extra responsibility and the few extra shillings he received in his pay.

Early on the morning of October 22, 1877 the sound of an explosion echoed out across the hills and valleys and brought housewives out into the street looking desperately to the pits where their husbands and sons were working, not knowing from where the blast had come. Clouds of smoke filled the sky. After a few minutes the shouting died down and the women, and men who had been roused from their sleep after working the night shift, could see the surrounding mines, those in which they worked in the Muirkirk area, were not affected.

News quickly spread that fire damp had been present in Pits number two and three at the Blantyre Colliery, nine miles south of the city of Glasgow, and it shook the ground for miles around. It had been ignited by a naked flame. One hundred and twenty-six men had gone down number two pit and 107 down number three at 5.30am. The explosion killed 207 miners, the youngest a boy of just 11. The accident left 92 widows and 250 fatherless children. Rescue provisions were hopelessly inadequate. President of the Miners' National Association, and a former miner himself, Alexander Macdonald MP, prevented surviving employees from attempting a rescue on safety grounds for fear of more lives being lost.

A strange quiet settled over the miners' rows for miles around as the Blantyre disaster, the worst in Scotland's mining history, was discussed and plans put into action to help the families bury their dead and comfort them as best they could.

The impact of the explosion hit George particularly hard as he knew the dangers of his job as Fireman. He hadn't told Mary about this particular responsibility as they didn't discuss his work. She knew it was dangerous but she had faith that her husband would be careful and come home to her each day. The Blantyre explosion hit all the families hard and it was a reminder of not only the dangers and hardship faced by mine workers across the country, but their dependence on the mines for their wages and houses.

There was always someone who needed extra food or clothes, someone who could use a little extra money and Mary helped out wherever she could with whatever she could spare. After all, that someone was just as likely to be her next time around.

Six months after the accident, mine owners William Dixon Ltd raised summonses against 34 widows whose husbands had been killed at Blantyre and who had not left the tied miners' houses which they and their husbands had rented from the mining company. The women and their families were evicted on May 28, 1878. Mine workers and their families across Ayrshire felt the sting of this callous action, but they also knew the realities – the houses in which they lived belonged to the mine owners, and when there was not a miner living in the house, the affected families had to move on and make way for other workers.

Life was hard, there was no doubt, and Mary prayed for her husband and young family every day. She prayed that George would be spared injury or worse in the mines and she prayed that her children would never see the inside of a coal mine. Somehow - she didn't know how - she would steer her children into other occupations. If she was harder on her children about getting their lessons learned than some other mothers, she made no apologies for it. Despite the generations behind her of coal miners in the family, she had decided that she would work with every ounce of strength in her body to keep her remaining children safe. There would be no mines for them.

Chapter 17 (1879)

A NEW ANDREW

Another cold Christmas passed in the little house at Main Street, Muirkirk. Work came and went, and the fortunes of the McMurdos went up and down. The constant cold and damp meant the children always had colds and Mary did what she could to eke out an existence with the money George was able to bring into the household, but it wasn't easy, especially when the men didn't know if they'd have work from one week to the next.

It seemed that there would never be enough money, but life went on and in February Mary knew she was pregnant with her seventh child. Her eldest son Thomas, now 14, was almost old enough to start work in the mines, but she wanted to keep him in school for as long as she could. She could see the toll the mine conditions were taking on her husband and in her heart she knew that she didn't want any of her children to go down below.

Jane, now 12, was a great help and constant source of support to her mother as she helped her care for the younger children, Douglas now 6 and the second Wee Margaret now 2. The thought of another baby filled her with dread, and joy, as she wondered how they could continue to battle cramped conditions and disease. But she knew that she had to be strong for her family. There was no time to show any weakness. There was food to put on the table, clothes to wash and mend and nurturing to be done. Mary, at just 33, looked like a woman much older but she didn't have time to worry about her looks. The morning sickness seemed to lessen with each pregnancy, so much so that she battled on carrying heavy pails of water and coal, even though the new life within her needed her to slow down.

In mid-Autumn of 1879, George and Mary's seventh child was born in the little house in Main Street, Muirkirk. He was strong and healthy and born at full term.

"Three lads and two lassies," George said softly as he watched his wife cradle their new-born son in her arms. "Another Andrew Stevenson McMurdo?," he enquired of his wife.

"Aye," Mary said. "Another Andrew Stevenson McMurdo. Your mother will be pleased."

They now had two children named after George's mother's side of the family – Margaret Stevenson McMurdo and Andrew Stevenson McMurdo – and two children names after Mary's mother's side of the family – Jane Percy McMurdo and Douglas Percy McMurdo. Their eldest child Thomas had been named for his Grandfather McMurdo. They were now a family of 7 again.

By Christmas 1879, all five Christmas stockings were in use again and while Mary did her best to make it a happy Christmas for them all, there was little money to spare and the children had to make do with the knitted gloves and scarves their mother had made and a few toys their Grandfather Thomas had carved for them out of bits of branches he'd found in the woods. But they were loved and the children cared for little more than the food provided, a warm fire, a warm bed and a warm cuddle at night. They had many friends in the miners' row and the neighbourhood children shared their skipping ropes and marbles – well, most of the time they shared as there were fights as well, usually among the young boys, but it was brought on more by a sense of frustration and boredom than any real malice. Their fathers drank to kill the physical pain of hard labour and the mental anguish of making barely enough money to feed their growing families. Their mothers gossiped about anyone who was considered to be 'less well off' either morally or materially for it made them feel more in control of their busy lives, if just for a moment. Community spirit grew from the commonality of their lives, and a lack of privacy. There were no plans, no dreams and very little hope of ever having more than an adequate day-to-day existence. Times were tough, there was no doubt about it.

Chapter 18 (1881)

FOR AULD LANG SYNE

R egardless of the lack of money, the men always seemed to find enough to buy whisky or ale to take a skinful at hogmanay. In the cold light of day there was little to celebrate about their lives, but at the end of one year and the start of a new year, through the fog of alcohol there was always hope for better times to come. Grandfather Thomas McMurdo, now 65, still enjoyed a dram with his friends and sons. His wife Margaret did not share his passion for the drink but she didn't want to take away one of his few pleasures in life and, while she lectured him often on the demons of drink, she mostly turned a blind eye when he came home a little under the weather, or went visiting friends, as he often did now.

With *Auld Lang Syne* still ringing in his ears from the night before's hogmanay celebrations, usually Thomas would be off to his work at the pit, but it was a rare day off from the mines and he was up and about his work around the house which these days consisted of carrying in the coal and water, reflective time sitting by the fire gazing into its flames and whittling pieces of wood, and taking long walks.

They had moved in recent years from Railway Terrace Muirkirk as Thomas followed the work and were now in a little house at another miners' row. Connel Park at New Cumnock consisted of 104 houses, mostly made of stone, which had been built to attract miners from other coalfields to work the coal reserves in the area. About 500 people lived in the Connel Park miners' row and the McMurdos lived at number 7. Life for Grandfather Thomas and Granny Margaret was lonely after so many years of their house being filled to the brim with laughter and tears, illness and fears.

While Margaret enjoyed the stillness of the quiet little house, it drove Thomas to distraction. With the children gone, even though they all visited often, the couple had little to talk about.

Soon after his midday meal of bread, jam and tea Thomas rose from the kitchen table. On the way to the door he pulled his cloth cap from the peg on the wall and called to Margaret over his shoulder.

"I'm away to Old Cumnock now Maggie," he said.

"Mind you stay sober enough to find your way home, Thomas McMurdo," Margaret cautioned as his hand reached the knob on the door.

"Aye. I'll say hello to Auld Willie for ye," he said.

"Never heed Auld Willie," Margaret snapped. "He'll lead ye astray, that one. Look oot for yoursel'."

"Oh, aye," Thomas said absent-mindedly as he lifted the latch on the door.

"Are you no forgettin' something?," Margaret asked as he took his first tentative step out of the door. Thomas stopped and turned slowly as he looked at his wife still sitting at the table sipping tea.

"Oh, aye," he said again as he nodded his head and walked quickly back to the table to place a small kiss on his wife's cheek, before taking off again like a schoolboy who had just evaded trouble.

"Take care, old man," Margaret called after him and as the door shut behind him, she smiled to herself. It seemed their productive days were behind them now. Thomas still worked in the mines but he was old and frail and couldn't do the work he used to do, so his hours had been cut. He busied himself as best he could. Margaret on the other hand still had her work to do keeping house but her load was lightened from the days when she had cared for a house full of children. Still, she was always available to help all her children with their children, especially George and Mary who had suffered such great losses. She still had plenty to do.

In Old Cumnock, Thomas and his friend Willie shared a pleasant afternoon together, reminiscing about their earlier days in the mines, the men they had known and, when Willie's wife was not in earshot, the women they wish they had known. The afternoon turned into night and after giving Thomas his evening meal, Willie's wife turned him out into the night about 8 o'clock with a warning that he'd best make his way back to his wife.

Thomas left Willie's house, turned up his collar against the cold, and walked the short distance to the river which was full after recent heavy rains. He lit his pipe, sat down on a large rock and marvelled at the sight of the full moon shining on the snowy branches of the trees that lined the Ayr River, and the river itself so clear and clean in the moonlight. The whisky soaked through his thin, bony body and he felt happy and peaceful. As he lifted himself from the rock, humming a familiar tune, he slipped and fell into the river. His pipe fell from his mouth and his cap slipped from his head. The river was deep but he fought to stay afloat as the freezing water slapped him into sobriety. The cold, deep river dragged him down and his cries went unheard. Thomas held the breath in his coal-stained lungs and tried to rise to the surface but he was no swimmer. He fought with every ounce of strength left in his old body until a stillness engulfed him. Then he closed his eyes in surrender as he plunged to the murky depths. His life on this earth had ended – and the pain for his family had just begun.

Chapter 19 (1881)

A CAP AND A PIPE

At midnight, Granny Margaret awoke in her bed and realised that Thomas was not yet home. She lit a candle to give the house some light for when he stumbled in the door, as he had so many times before, but the candle burned down and soon it was morning with still no sign of her husband. Thomas had never stayed out all night. Somehow he'd always made it home.

Margaret quickly dressed and caught a ride with a passing horse and cart that took her the six miles to her son George's house at Main St, Muirkirk.

"Your faither's no come hame and I'm afeared for him," she told her son as he answered her anxious rapping on the door.

"Where was he going last night?," George enquired.

"To Auld Willie's hoose."

"Right then, you stay here with Mary and I'll fetch Thomas and William and we'll go into Old Cumnock. Dinnae fash yoursel' mither, we'll find him," George consoled his mother.

"Oh Geordy," Margaret said as she grabbed her son's arm. "I've got a bad feeling. He's never stayed away before."

George gently freed himself from his mother's grip and set off to fetch his two younger brothers. Together they hopped an early morning milk cart to take them the nine miles from Muirkirk into Old Cumnock and found Auld Willie's house from the description their mother had given them. When they knocked at the door of the white, stone cottage Willie's wife answered. Had she seen their father, George enquired.

"Aye, I fed him and turned him oot aboot 8 o'clock last night. Did he no' make it hame?," she asked.

"No," replied George, "and our mither's worried sick." By this time, Auld Willie was at the door scratching his balding head.

"He may have stopped somewhere to sleep. I'll come wi' ye and we'll have a look aboot," said the old man.

The four men split up, Auld Willie taking the nearby streets of Old Cumnock, with Thomas and William setting off on the road back to Connel Park that their father would have taken, while George was drawn to the river. He searched under bushes and in wood piles in the hope that his father had decided to take a sleep until the drink wore off. As he neared an outcrop of rocks his heart skipped a beat. Lying there, muddied and half-buried, was his father's well-worn cloth cap. George picked up the cap and held it to his breast.

"Oh faither," he whispered, "where can ye be?" He began to scan the river and something caught his eye off to the left. George walked a few paces, bent down and unearthed the pipe that was never far from his father's lips.

Suddenly he stood up and began shouting to whoever was in earshot, "over here, come over here, I've found somethin'."

The men ran to his side as George's eyes dashed up and down the river in the hope of finding his father nearby. For two hours George and his brothers, accompanied by Auld Willie and some neighbouring men, scoured the banks of the Ayr River but no further sign of Thomas was found.

The boys trudged wearily home, using the long walk to discuss how they would tell their mother. As they all arrived at George's house, Mary was baking bread while her mother-in-law Margaret was busying herself playing with her grandchildren. The door opened and there stood her three eldest sons. She knew by the looks on their faces that Thomas was not with them. Then she saw the muddied piece of cloth that George was clutching in his strong, right hand. As she looked from George's face to the cloth and back again, she realised that it was Thomas's cap he was holding. Margaret rose quickly from her chair and moved towards George. She snatched the cloth from her son's hand and held it up to the light. It was Thomas's cap all right, the one she had seen him take down from the peg near the door every day for the past 20-odd years, and she held it to her bosom. Then George pulled the mud-caked pipe from his pocket and handed it to her apologetically.

"We found these by the river, mither," he began, seeing no point in shielding her from the truth. "We've searched for hours but we're no' givin' up hope. We've come back to get Tommy, John, Rab and Davey and as many men as we can gather to continue the search." It hurt George to see the pain in his mother's eyes. She began to rock back and forth and he caught her before her tired body hit the floor. He scooped her up in his arms and lay her gently on the bed as his Mary prepared a cold compress for Margaret's head. Knowing that she was in good hands, George, William and Thomas set off to find their brothers and they returned to Old Cumnock.

For the next three days they searched with every spare minute they had but it soon became clear that their father would not be coming back.

Lizzie, heavily pregnant with her second child, took the news badly. As soon as her brother George arrived at the door of her miner's cottage with the news, Lizzie dressed her two-year-old daughter Margaret in a warm coat and went with George to his house to be with their mother. Lizzie had had a special relationship with her father Thomas and she idolised him. Before marrying her husband James, her father was the man she loved with all her heart and couldn't wait to see him after his shift at the mines. She had loved looking after him, bringing him water and soap to clean away the grime. And oh how he'd wanted her to have more than he could give her. "My Lizzie will be a fine lady with ribbons and lace" Thomas had told his little girl. On the walk to George's house she thought of the fun times she'd had with her father. She remembered dancing around the little kitchen of their house with him when he'd come home with a few drinks under his belt, and hearing him sing after supper sometimes. Her baby was due in just a few weeks and she wanted her father to know this child. She prayed that he would be found and refused to believe that there could be any other outcome.

Chapter 20 (1881)

A GRUESOME FIND

The seaside town of Ayr had become a highly fashionable resort from the early 1800s, most notably because of the steamer services, and then the railway came in 1840 linking Ayr with nearby Prestwick and Glasgow. Ayr Harbour was a busy, deep waterway that attracted a lot of foreign vessels. The banks of the Ayr were home to shipbuilders and the river itself was home to whitefish and salmon, adding to the town's economy as a fishing port. The Ayr River was always busy with fishing boats, coal vessels and dredgers working in the harbour to make it deep enough to attract even bigger ships.

On January 24, the dredger *Ayr* had been working in the harbour about 100 feet from the North Quay wall, opposite the foot of Green Street. At about 5 o'clock in the afternoon, in preparation for knocking off work, the men of the dredger hoisted the silt lifting machinery out of the water. The master of the dredger, known to all as Big Billy, had been supervising the last-minute preparations as he eagerly awaited the shift to be over so that he could wash away the salt in his throat down at the Market Inn. With a look of horror on his weather-worn face, Big Billy called out to his foreman to stop the lift.

With his hand in the air as though this very action was all that was holding the lift, he moved closer to the buckets on the lifting machinery.

"Is that what I think it is?," he said to no one in particular. There, wedged between two of the buckets was the leg of a man which apparently had been torn by the buckets off a body lying in the bed of the river.

"Call the Polis," Big Billy said to his foreman who ran from the dredger to the Ayr Police Station. "You men stay on board till the Polis get here," he instructed his crew.

When the police sergeant arrived on board the dredger, he ordered that the leg be removed and taken to the local hospital. Big Billy assigned two of his men the grim task of retrieval and sat down with the sergeant.

"You know, there could be more," he began as the earnest young police sergeant took notes in his book.

"More…people. Do you think there could be people at the bottom of the Ayr Harbour?," he said excitedly.

"Ah, well maybe not people but a person perhaps. Aboot 1 o'clock today I saw what I thought were animal remains brought up in the buckets and emptied into the punts, but that often happens so I thought nothin' of it," said Big Billy, rubbing his giant hand across his stubbled chin.

"You often find remains?," asked the earnest young sergeant.

"Aye," said Big Billy, "but they're usually animals that get in the way o' the teeth o' the buckets. We take the punts out and empty them into the bay."

"But you're thinking now that the remains were not from an animal?," asked the sergeant as he continued to scribble with a stunted pencil in his book.

"Well, it stands to reason do you no' think," said Big Billy, "it would have been the remains of the body of the man whose leg we just found." Billy ran his meaty fingers through his greasy black hair as he became frustrated with the sergeant.

The sergeant nodded earnestly.

"Can I let my men go now, sergeant," asked Big Billy as his men began to shift about restlessly.

"Aye, let them go but I want a list of all their names and addresses taken to the police station. There'll no doubt be an enquiry."

When the sergeant returned to the Police Station he could not find a missing person's report for anyone in the district but as his enquiries broadened, he could come to only one conclusion.

Later that night he found himself on the doorstep of the McMurdo home in Connel Park. It had been just over three weeks since Thomas had gone missing and his wife Margaret had dragged herself through each long day. Her sons and daughters took turns to be with her and on this day, her eldest son George was with her. He opened the door to see the police sergeant standing with his helmet under his left arm.

"I'm looking for a Mrs Margaret Stevenson McMurdo," said the sergeant.

"Aye, ye'll find her here," said George as he moved back from the doorway. "Ye'd better come in."

Margaret sat up from the bed where she had been resting as George asked the sergeant to sit down at the table. George put his hand under his mother's elbow and lead her to the table.

"Mrs McMurdo," the sergeant began, "we have some news. It's not good I'm afraid. In fact," he said tentatively, "it's quite grim. Would you like me to speak with your son alone?"

Margaret felt numb and had prepared herself for the day that someone would knock at her door to tell her that her husband was dead.

"Speak plainly to me sergeant," Margaret said as she straightened her back in the chair. "Have ye found our Thomas?"

The sergeant hesitated. "Well, yes – and no. That is to say, we believe we may have but we can't be sure."

"For God's sake spit it oot, man," George said impatiently.

"Brace yourself Mrs McMurdo," the sergeant said as he began to read from his book. "This afternoon, at approximately 5 o'clock the men of the Ayr dredger were finishing up for the day when they noticed something caught between two buckets." He looked up from his notebook briefly and continued. "It was the leg of a man and as no one has been reported missing in the district, and on enquiry around the area, I can only conclude that it is the leg of your missing husband, Thomas McMurdo. Even though you didn't file a missing person's report, he is the only person, officially or unofficially missing in the past three weeks, according to my enquiries around about. And...," he hesitated.

George looked at him urging him to complete his grim errand. "And as the body has apparently not been long in the water, the most likely supposition is that the body is that of one Thomas McMurdo."

There it was. The news they had all feared, but knew to be true, had been delivered. Thomas was gone and not even a body to bury.

"Er, what do we, well I mean, how do we - what happens now," George stammered.

"Well, usually when a body is found, and when it is still possible, we require a family member to make a formal identification and a post-mortem examination is conducted. Then there is usually an enquiry to find out the cause of death. In this instance, well, er, we will require a family member to identify the leg," said the sergeant as he lowered his eyes to the ground.

Margaret, George and the earnest young sergeant sat together in the little house. The candles flickered and the fire crackled but all around them was an unearthly stillness.

Suddenly the silence was shattered as George slammed his hand down on the table decisively.

"Right then," he said as he rose from the table and ushered the sergeant towards the door. "I'll bring some of my brothers to Ayr tomorrow morning. Good night to you."

As the door closed, George swallowed hard and turned towards his mother Margaret still seated at the table staring into the fire.

"Gather up your shawl mither," he said. "You're coming home with me tonight and you'll stay with Mary tomorrow when the lads and I go to Ayr."

Margaret was silent and obediently followed her eldest son's instructions. For the moment she could not think and was happy for someone else to do the thinking for her. Her Thomas was gone. Her happiness was gone. Her heart was broken.

Once his mother was settled, George had the unpleasant task of spreading the news to his brothers and sisters. He dreaded telling his sister Lizzie the grim news. She opened the door to her house with her week-old son in her arms. The stress had been too much for her and baby Andrew Sheddon Howie had been born a little early on January 18.

"He's no' comin' hame, lass," was all George could say. Lizzie held her son close to her and her husband James lead her to a wooden chair by the fire – one of a pair of chairs that her father Thomas had given her when she married. She sat for a moment then handed the baby to James, got up from her chair, walked to the mantle place and picked up a small wooden box. She slowly opened the box and took out a thin red ribbon – the ribbon her father Thomas had used to tie up the little green box containing the silver thistle brooch that he had given her mother for Christmas all those years ago. She fondled the ribbon between her fingers, looked at her eldest brother standing helplessly in the doorway, ran to him and held him tight. George kissed her gently on her forehead, pulled away from her embrace and left for home. He had a big day ahead of him.

On the morning of January 25, 1882 the four eldest sons of Thomas McMurdo - George, Thomas, William and James – set off from Muirkirk for Ayr by train to try to make a positive identification of their father's remains. They reached the mortuary and were taken to a table covered by a white sheet. The mortuary attendant lifted the sheet to reveal a leg, clothed in a sock and portions of trousers and drawers. Between them the lads believed that the items of clothing were similar to those worn by their father.

On the official report, the mortuary attendant wrote: "Four of the deceased's sons came to Ayr this morning and examined the remains. They state that the sock and portions of trousers and drawers are similar to those worn by their father. They expect that the tailor who made the trousers, and their mother who repaired the sock, will be able to speak more definitely on the subject."

Their mother Margaret was never consulted about the sock.

Chapter 21 (1881)

GONE BUT NOT FORGOTTEN

The McMurdo family set about grieving their loss. The story made the front page of the *Ayr Advertiser* and word got around that Thomas had drowned. He was well known in the district, as much for his penchant for bursting into song after a few drinks at The Black Bull as for his kindly ways and large family of strong, sturdy sons.

With no body to bury, Thomas's sons decided that their father's life would still be celebrated. Margaret arranged for Reverend MacKelvie to perform a special memorial service for Thomas, and his eight adult sons - George 41, Thomas 39, William 36, James 32, John 29, Robert 25, David 23 and Andrew almost 18 - organised a wake at The Black Bull for his family, friends and co-workers. His daughters Lizzie, 27, and her two small children, newly-married Mary 19 and Margaret 18, comforted their mother as best they could, but the passing of Thomas had left a hole in all their lives.

A couple of weeks later, on February 17, an inquest into the death of Thomas McMurdo, Pit Bottomer aged 65, was held but as no evidence was found as to his disappearance, the cause of death was proclaimed as 'supposed drowning' as the result of a precognition signed off by the registrar W B Cuthbertson.

Margaret erected a headstone in Muirkirk Cemetery in memory of her husband. With no husband and no income, she would have to rely on the generosity of her children for her very livelihood, but she still had many years of work left in her, she felt, and could be of use in helping with her grandchildren. Her sons David and Andrew, both coal miners, still lived at home so at least she still had a roof over her head. She put on her black mourning clothes and prepared to live the life of a widow, staying indoors for a year and a day as was the custom, and as a mark of respect to her beloved husband. She would put on a happy face for her family and leave her crying until she was alone in her bed. She prayed that Thomas would visit her in her dreams.

Chapter 22 (1883)

LIFE AFTER LOSS

After all the upset of the past couple of years and with the bizarre death and finding of his father Thomas, George found himself once more helping his mother Margaret deal with her grief. Her seventh-born son David, known to the family as Davey, a coal miner like his father, contracted Miner's Lung and died at Glengyron Row, aged just 25, on June 12, 1883. George sat with his younger brother as he battled the disease that claimed the lives of so many of the men who worked underground. He had seen men come to work wracked with coughing fits as they tried to expel the thick black phlegm that had built up in their lungs overnight, then pick up their tools and head down into the dust for another ten hours. The disease weakened many a man and his brother, so young, had succumbed to its eventual fate.

After his brother's funeral, and knowing that his mother Margaret was being cared for by her youngest son Andrew who was still at home, and the rest of the family, George could once again concentrate on his own family. At age 43, he felt years older and his shoulders were stooped from the yoke of responsibility he felt to his growing family and the years spent down the mines working in spaces no higher than three feet. He stood in the street outside his house, then leaned against the cold stone as he sucked on his pipe, and reflected on the past few years. His wife Mary was happy again after suffering so greatly from the loss of their five-month-old baby Andrew eight years before and the further loss of their six-year-old daughter Margaret just five months later. Since then, their sixth child, also called Margaret, had been born in 1877 and their seventh child, also called Andrew, had been born in 1879. Now Mary was well pregnant with their eighth child.

George suffered from the guilt of many of the men in the miners' rows. The guilt of living from day to day and pay to pay, of not being able to provide a better house for his family and more food on the table. It pained him to watch his children clothed in worn-out dresses and trousers and to see his beloved Mary, once so young and full of life, reduced to a life of making do. God knows, his mother-in-law had reminded him many times of his inadequacies as a husband, but Mary never complained. She just got on with what had to be done and despite a lack of money and possessions, she ensured that the children went to school clean and that there was food, no matter how insubstantial, on the table for them each night. The children knew how to use a knife and fork even though they may never get the chance to use their table manners in public, and they were read to every night by the fire or told stories of times past.

As he took his last draw from the pipe and gently whacked it against his hand to empty out the ash, he saw a willowy figure coming towards him with a basket over her arm. She had a spring in her step that reminded him of his sister Lizzie when she was younger. Her long, blonde hair cascaded around her shoulders as she held her head high the way her mother Mary had always done as she walked down the street.

"What are ye doing out here in the cold faither," asked his 16-year-old daughter Jane as she returned from visiting a friend. "You'll catch yer death."

"Just watching the passing parade, Janie," said George. "Watching the time go by."

"Oh, faither, you've more to do surely than let time pass ye by. Every day should be an adventure."

"Oh, Janie," Thomas said solemnly, "promise me you'll always keep that attitude. Don't let anyone ever crush yer spirit."

"No fear of that, faither," Janie said as she took her father by the arm and led him inside the house. "I have my own mind."

100

George smiled and thought to himself, 'there's a lot of my Mary in our Janie'.

Mary looked on admiringly as her husband and daughter walked into the house arm in arm, sharing a laugh. There was Janie, almost a young woman, and here Mary was with another child on the way. She wanted to love this baby and she was determined that she would. The rawness of loss had subsided somewhat but she always held a little of herself in reserve, almost afraid to love in case she was hurt again. She had held her love from George for a long time after she lost the children, but now their love would produce another child. She wondered what sort of a life her wean would be born into.

Chapter 23 (1883)

AND BABY MAKES EIGHT

In August, in the Summer of 1883, George and Mary McMurdo's eighth child was born. He was christened William after Mary's father William Hamilton. With the loss of wee Margaret and baby Andrew, the family now consisted of six children and their parents, crammed into the little house in Main Street Muirkirk.

The joy of the new child was diminished by the death of Mary's mother Jane Hamilton on May 1 that same year. Though they had had their differences, Mary had become close to her mother and would miss their many afternoon teas together. She had been a stern, reserved old woman but Mary loved her, for all her airs and graces. Mary's father had been a gentle soul, but he too was gone. In the 20 years since her marriage to George, Mary had known the joys and sadness of being a wife and mother and when her own mother passed, she began to realise that the woman who had caused her so much consternation had had her share of troubles too. "Life makes people the way they are", Mrs Hamilton had always said, and Mary was beginning to realise the truth in that statement. Her mother had known hard times but she managed to put on a brave face and act as though the troubles of life just passed her by. It was a good act. Mary knew that now. Her mother's preoccupation with everyone else's business had been her way of taking her mind off her own troubles. In reflective moments Mary remembered her mother with fondness, the way a mother should be remembered.

She prayed that her own children would remember her that way – as a loving mother who, despite all her perceived frailties, did her best while trying to keep body and soul together.

For now Mary was happy with her bouncing new baby and the love of her husband and children.

Chapter 24 (1884)

THE JOY IS SHORT-LIVED

Work in the pits was more often than not interrupted by strike action these days and men being layed off by the mine owners. No work meant no house or coal for their fireplaces, and many families lived pay to pay, without the most basic of comforts of the poverty-stricken – a warm fire. George had to follow the work and late in 1883 the family moved to a miners' row in Cumnock. At 8 Glengyron Row, about a mile from Old Cumnock, there were 44 apartment houses. The kitchen measured 15 feet by 12 feet and the other room about 10 feet by 9 feet, similar to most of the other miners' rows in which they had lived. This row was also owned by William Baird and Co.

After living for many years in Main Street Muirkirk, and losing the first baby Andrew and the first wee Margaret in that house, Mary was glad to move. The family settled in, with Mary and her daughter Jane cleaning the new place from top to bottom and making the younger children Douglas 10, Margaret 5, Andrew 4, and baby William as comfortable as possible. Elder son Thomas, despite his mother's protestations, now worked with his father George in the mines. There were few work options for the young people in and around Old Cumnock. He was 18 and brought in an extra pay packet, and they needed every penny from the two men's wages to survive.

Thomas had a box bed in the kitchen, where Andrew, Douglas and Jane also slept on another box bed, while Margaret had a little bed in her parents' room and baby William slept in his cradle.

At the end of October as the rain poured down and the little house became damp, Mary noticed that (the second) wee Margaret had a persistent cough. As Autumn turned into Winter and the rain turned snow into slush, the house became colder and damper and the three younger children began to cough throughout the night. Mary was worried about baby William but after a week his cough stopped and he seemed to thrive. Douglas and Andrew, though thin and pale, recovered well also but Mary was worried about wee Margaret. She had lost weight and wasn't eating. She became tired and listless and coughed constantly.

Mary and George watched as their little girl suffered coughing fits and failed to improve.

"We've got to call a doctor, George," Mary said anxiously. "I don't care how much it costs. The school is nearly empty of children all with the coughing fits and that's where she's got it. I can't see her suffer."

"Aye, I'll fetch the doctor," George said as he hastened out the door into the snow and driving rain.

Doctor James Morrison arrived at Glengyron Row in his horse and buggy. He examined Margaret and told her mother to try to feed her broth and keep her warm.

"There is little I can do Mrs McMurdo," Dr Morrison said flatly. He had delivered that line to so many families in the past few months and he was devoid of emotion. "I suspect that Margaret has contracted tuberculosis at school from other children coughing and sneezing." He looked around the little house and continued: "and the damp and crowded conditions here in the miners' rows are not ideal for a speedy recovery."

Mary looked at the doctor, unable to take in what he was saying. Swallowing hard, she replied: "I do my best to keep the house clean Doctor, and my children are fed the best food we can afford," she said indignantly.

"For goodness sake woman, I'm not blaming you for your child's condition," chastised Dr Morrison. "This disease is claiming lives all over Scotland and as a physician I can tell you that I am frustrated because there is not a thing I can do about it."

Mary regained her composure. Handing the doctor his hat, she said: "Thank you doctor, how much do I owe you?" Looking around the little house again, the doctor said: "Oh, two shillings and sixpence." Mary reached into the little blue cloth bag that she'd had for many years and pulled out some coins. Handing them to the doctor she said: "I believe the normal cost of a doctor's visit is four shillings, and four shillings you shall have," and she thrust the money into his hands. She walked to the door and opened it, then stood still and said: "good day to you Doctor," and Dr Morrison left quietly. He admired her courage and pride. Like most of the families in the miners' rows, Mary had little money to spare, but she would never accept charity and even though she needed every penny, she had insisted on paying him the full amount of his fee. He drove off in his horse and buggy marvelling at the strength and courage of this coal miner's wife.

Over the next few weeks Mary and George watched as their tiny, six-year-old daughter became weaker. She complained of sore arms and legs and began to cough up blood.

It was then that Mary realised there could be no good outcome. Each night as she lay in bed, she prayed that her child would get better. She saw the face of the daughter she had also called Margaret Stevenson McMurdo, and relived the anguish of the child's last weeks on earth. As Mary lay there in the dark, pleading with God to spare her child, she heard wee Margaret gasp. She lit the candle that rested on the ledge beside her bed and woke George. As she moved the candle closer, she could see blood coming from Margaret's mouth and as George lifted her up to a sitting position, Margaret's eyes rolled back in her head and her body went limp. As the tears streamed down George's face, Mary fell to her knees in stunned silence, eyes wide with fear, but still tightly clutching the candle. Woken by the light of the candle, son Thomas was quickly by her side. As he knelt down to help his mother he looked across at the sight of his strong, silent father sobbing uncontrollably as he held the tiny body of Margaret in his arms.

"She's gone," was all he could say over and over. "Our wee lassie's gone."

Mary looked up to see Jane holding baby William, with Douglas and Andrew huddled together in the doorway as they took in the tragic scene.

Thomas motioned to Douglas to hold on to his mother who was still kneeling on the floor by Margaret's bed, as he went to fetch Doctor Morrison. Before he left the house, he went to the mantle and stopped the clock at 10.15pm, as was the custom, to mark the time of death.

Mary and George and the children were sitting at the kitchen table when the doctor arrived, accompanied by a midwife. He had seen it many times before - a child lying dead in her bed - but it never got easier for him. He examined wee Margaret and pronounced her dead on March 19, 1884. As the doctor set about writing the death certificate, the midwife bathed Margaret's emaciated body and layed her out ready for viewing.

Though the McMurdo family was reasonably new to Glengyron Row the women felt a kinship as they were bonded in sorrow. So many children in the district had fallen victim to tuberculosis and they understood Mary's loss. They comforted her as best they could, but she once again retreated into her shell and was determined not to let anyone near her heart again.

George and his eldest son Thomas carried wee Margaret's coffin from the house at 8 Glengyron Row to the church before moving on to the kirkyard to lay her to rest.

Mary's pain was written on her stoney face, but George carried his pain within, trying to be strong and hold his family together in the face of such sorrow. Whereas Mary could scream and shout and not allow herself to love or be loved as she dealt with her fear and aching, George bottled it all up and ached from within.

'Eight children', he thought to himself as he stood at the grave, 'and three of them buried here'. He looked across the hole in the ground that contained his daughter's coffin, at his remaining

children. 'God, take me before you take another one of them,"
he offered up as a silent prayer. 'It's not right that a father
should bury his children. Please, if you've to take anyone, take
me.'

Chapter 25 (1885)

THE MINER'S CURSE

After burying their second wee Margaret, once again the only mirror in the house was covered in black cloth, and it mattered not to Mary for she could not bear to look at herself. The children were sad at the loss of their sister, George suffered in silence and Mary's heart grew colder. The family struggled to recover. Tuberculosis was rife throughout Scotland and the cramped, dusty and wet conditions in which the miners and their families were forced to live made it difficult for anyone who contracted an illness to recover quickly. The working conditions of the men down the mines were also damp, dusty and dangerous. While George watched over Mary and his children for signs of depression and illness, his own health started to decline. The impure air in which he was forced to work irritated his airways and for some months he had suffered from chronic bronchitis. During the night secretions would build up in his lungs and each morning started with a coughing fit until the troublesome mucus could be expelled. Everyone in the McMurdo household except Mary had coughs and colds – it had become part of life as the rain and snow caused rising damp in their little house and the coal fires struggled to keep them all warm.

By August, George's condition had worsened and he began to experience tightness in his chest and difficulty in breathing. The constant headaches and aching limbs meant that he often missed a day's work, which the family could scarcely afford, and this played heavily on his mind. Early in November, as George struggled to breathe, Mary called for the doctor. George knew before the doctor could speak. He'd watched his own brother Davey suffer not two years before. He had seen many men over his years in the mines go down with Miner's Lung, their lungs so choked with black phlegm that they were drowning in their own bodily fluids. He knew exactly what was wrong with him, but he'd passed it off to Mary as just a bad cold. 'The poor lass has suffered enough,' he thought, 'she doesn't need to know the worst just yet.'

The doctor took out his stethoscope and listened to George's fast heartbeat and heavy lungs. As he threw back the bedclothes he saw George's emaciated body, the shrivelled skin and prominent veins on his arms and his waxy complexion.

Mary looked on anxiously with two-year-old William fidgeting on her hip, as the new surgeon in the village Dr Granger completed his examination. Then, putting his stethoscope back into his small, black bag he sat down on the little stool beside George's bed.

"You've got Pthisis Pulmonalis, George," the doctor said.

"Aye, it's Miner's Lung," George said breathlessly. "I know that Doctor."

"What can we do for him, Doctor?" Mary asked.

"He needs clean, fresh water and whatever food he can take which will probably be just a broth. I won't lie to you Mrs McMurdo," the doctor continued. "If he was a few years younger the prognosis might be better, but in my experience men over 40 who contract Phtisis…er…Miner's Lung don't handle it well. All you can do is keep him comfortable."

"Are you saying what I think you're saying, Doctor?," Mary asked quickly. "You can't be saying that Doctor, you just can't!"

The Doctor looked at George who was too weak to be of much use to his beloved Mary, then reached into his bag and gave Mary a tot of medicine 'to calm her nerves'.

"I'll come back tomorrow," the Doctor said.

Mary placed little William on a bed in the kitchen to play with a carved wooden horse that his grandfather had made some years before, then lay down beside her husband George and held his

110

hand. They had been married for 22 years and she couldn't bear to see it end. What of her dreams of them growing old together? How would she go on without him?

As George dozed, Mary questioned how much more pain she could take. 'My baby Andrew and the two wee Margarets, my mother Jane, my father William and now my man,' she thought. 'What have I done to deserve this? Why are you punishing me God?' she prayed silently. As her panic subsided, she looked over at her husband as the breath rattled out of his sleeping body and she knew that, once again, it wasn't about her. Her task now was to make the last days on earth of her beloved husband as comfortable as possible, and to prepare the children for the inevitable. She would be strong. She had to be.

As she moved from the bed to check on William, George stirred from his sleep. He weakly reached out for her and she sat back down on the bed.

"It's not the life I'd hoped to give ye, lass," George whispered to Mary. "I fell in love with ye when we danced on the green all those years ago and I've never stopped loving ye." He paused to catch his breath. "And I'll go on loving ye."

"Save your breath, my Darling," Mary said as she brushed her hand gently across his brow.

"No, I need to tell ye…not to worry. Thomas will look after you all. And Dougie's a good lad. Even though he's still at school he can help. And you've got our Janie for company." His words trailed off as he launched into another coughing fit and sunk back into the pillow exhausted. Mary pulled the covers around him and stared into his thin face. She wanted to lie down beside him and have them fade away together.

Chapter 26 (1885)

A LIFE IN BLACK

A life spent down the pits earning a living, and the stress of not only trying to raise a family but seeing disease steal away three of his children, had taken its toll on George.

Exhausted from the disease that he had battled for 10 months, George McMurdo died on November 22, 1885 at 3.25pm in Glengyron Row, aged just 45. He was buried in the Muirkirk Cemetery with his children - Andrew and the two Margarets.

His mother Margaret had lost another son. At just 39 years of age, but looking much older, Mary was left to head up the household of Thomas, 20, Jane, 18, Douglas, 12, Andrew, 6, and William, 2. She dyed all her clothes black and prepared to live the rest of her life as a widow. Her outer appearance was as dark as her heart had become. She was in mourning for her beloved husband and still grieving from the loss of three children. Each day brought new trials and she walked in a daze through the chores she had to accomplish. Her life had become a hell on earth.

Chapter 27 (1886)

SOLIDARITY WITH KEIR HARDIE

With her husband's death from Miner's Lung, contracted after years spent down the pits, Mary was determined that her sons Douglas, Andrew and William would not be destined for a life working underground. Her eldest son Thomas had already followed his father into the mines and was showing an interest in the union movement that had begun to take hold in the Ayrshire mines. Thomas was an adult and could make up his own mind and Mary was grateful for the wages he brought in – it was what kept the family going. Miners' families received cheap rental on their houses and cheap coal for their fires and Mary was glad of that, but she worried every time Thomas left for a shift at the mine, just as she had worried the same way about her beloved husband George.

Thomas had the fiery nature that Mary had had when she was young – he was headstrong and opinionated and had ideas about improving the miners' lot. His grandfather Thomas and father George had had similar notions when they were young but, despite their desire for better working conditions and wages, they put the welfare of their large families first and valued a pay packet above all else. Thomas's lifestyle was not so constrained. Although he had the financial responsibility for his mother and four siblings, he was free to pursue his thoughts and associations for the betterment of himself and his fellow workers. He had seen his father and his Uncle Davey die from Miner's Lung and the suffering it brought to his family. Unnecessary suffering, he felt.

For Mary and her family, the time spent at Glengyron Row was short and not long after George died, the McMurdo family moved to a house in another mining community at Barrhill Road, Cumnock. While Thomas earned the wages for the household, Jane helped her mother keep house and look after young William, and Douglas and Andrew attended the local school. Mary was determined to keep her children at school as long as possible, to give them a good education that might fit them out for suitable employment.

The move to Barrhill Rd proved fortuitous for Thomas. Not a year after his father George had died, the Ayrshire Miners' Union was formed and James Keir Hardie, or Keir as he had become known, a long-time supporter of trade unions, was appointed secretary. Hardie also lived in Barrhill Rd and Thomas admired and respected this self-educated and passionate man. Hardie had started working 12-hour shifts in the mines at age 11 and had never been to school. His mother taught him to read and write. He began to read newspapers and found that some workers were attempting to improve their wages and working conditions by forming trade unions. Hardie helped to establish a union at his colliery and in 1880 led the first ever strike of Lanarkshire miners. This led to his dismissal and after moving to Old Cumnock the following year, the young man who could scarcely read or write until he was 17 years old, took up a job as a journalist on local newspaper *The Cumnock News*.

Thomas followed Hardie's call to action for an increase in wages and better working conditions, and the two became firm friends. The bushy beard and world-weary eyes gave Hardie a look of maturity beyond his 35 years. He and his wife Lillie - who was virtually raising their family alone while her husband followed his political pursuits - welcomed neighbours into their home and many a needy family found a bowl of soup at the Hardies' table. He had a genuine care and compassion for his fellow man and his charisma was a magnet for a young man like Thomas McMurdo whose own ambitions aligned with Hardie's.

The Miner newspaper which Hardie began publishing in 1887 could be found in most miners' homes and the talk among the men often turned to politics, whether they realised it or not. Continued accidents in the workplace only steeled the miners' resolve to take on the mine owners and demand improvements in safety.

On May 28, 1887, 73 miners died in a fire damp explosion at Udston Colliery, Hamilton. Keir Hardie, by then secretary of the Scottish Miners' Federation, denounced the deaths as murder and other miners, including young Thomas McMurdo, became even more determined to do something about improving safety in the pits. At 9am on the day of the explosion, the day shift miners at Udston Colliery downed tools for their breakfast, after having been hard at work since 6am. During this break, at 9.07am, an explosion ripped through the Splint Seam destroying everything in its path. The explosion manifested itself in a volume of flame and dust at the number two or downcast shaft, followed seconds later by a volume of flame from the upcast or number one shaft which set fire to the wooden sheds or headings above it.

The sound of the explosion was heard in neighbouring Greenfield Colliery through a 135-foot (41 m) barrier of solid coal. In the Blantyre Colliery (where an estimated 216 men had lost their lives 10 years earlier) miners working that morning were temporarily blinded with the dust thrown up by the vibration of the Udston Colliery explosion.

The 73 men who died at the Udston disaster were paid on average 3 shillings and 3 pence per day or 17 shillings and 6 pence per week – a pittance in exchange for their back-breaking work and ultimately, their lives.

On August 25, 1888 the Scottish Labour Party was inaugurated in Glasgow with Robert Bontine Cunninghame Graham as president and James Keir Hardie as secretary. Hardie's political career was well on its way and Thomas McMurdo and the other miners stood in solidarity with him as the ideal candidate to express the miners' grievances. Mine owners had long seen Hardie as an agitator and as he moved seamlessly from coal mines to union organisation work they realised that he was a force to be reckoned with.

As Thomas continued to financially sustain the McMurdo household, his mother Mary ran the home with a firm and guiding hand as always. Since her husband's death, Mary had found the strength that had previously deserted her. When her babies had died she had had George to lean on, but now she alone was responsible for the physical and moral welfare of her family and she took her duties very seriously.

In 1888 Douglas turned 15 and was ready to leave school. He could have had a job in the mines a year before but Mary was having none of that. She wanted him to find a trade and was successful in securing him an apprenticeship with the local baker. While Thomas provided cheap coal for the fires from his work in the pits, and was the main wage earner, it was Douglas who now became the 'bread' winner and kept the family in a steady supply of unsold bread and buns. He liked the work and he knew it made his mother happy to see him head off to work each day to a 'nice safe occupation'.

Jane was now a young woman of 20 and of marriageable age although she showed little interest in the passing glances of the young men as she walked the dusty streets of the village. She was fair and slim and her translucent skin had a muted glow about it. She was rarely without a book in her hand and could be found in her spare moments curled up in a corner reading romance novels. She had inherited her love of books from both her Aunt Lizzie and her mother Mary. Jane could have gone into service in a large estate but chose instead to remain in her mother's home to help her raise the family.

"You must think of the future Janie," her mother had told her.

"But I am content with my life and am happy today," she had said. "I have no thought for tomorrow."

Chapter 28 (1888)

ANOTHER LIGHT FADES

Perhaps it was prophetic that Jane didn't see a future for herself. In the Summer of 1888 Mary noticed that Jane had a persistent cough, and it struck fear into her heart. Though the address had changed, the living conditions hadn't and the house at Barrhill Road was also damp and mildewy, despite Mary's regimen of cleanliness. Over the next twelve months Jane's health deteriorated. She lost weight from her already slender frame and the much-admired pale translucent skin became a tell-tale sign that she was suffering from tuberculosis.

By the Spring of 1890 Jane was bedridden and weak and Mary began to accept what she hoped she would never have to face again. Her only surviving daughter would not live to know the joys of marriage or have a family of her own. In the last weeks of Jane's life, Mary read to her daughter, bathed her wasting body and tried to get some sustenance into her. She tried to give her own strength to her daughter and when Jane was able, they talked about life – and death.

"I know I'm not long for this world, mither," Jane said as she gazed into her mother's eyes. "Don't be afraid, for I am not. I know that faither and the two wee Margarets and baby Andrew will be waiting in heaven to greet me, so you see I'll no' be alone. It is you mither I worry for. It is you who has seen such loss and you've still so much work to do to raise Andrew and William. But if I can, I'll take some of the burden away from you. Just think of me and somehow I know that I'll be able to hear your thoughts and be by your side."

As Mary started to cry, Jane reached out for her hand. "Come now mither," she said. "Be brave."

Those two words from her beloved daughter cut Mary to the core. She knew she had to be brave, but she was tired of being brave, tired of accepting every cross that she had to bear. 'What harm has Janie ever done anyone,' she thought as she sat by Jane's bed one long, last night.

Tuberculosis had gained the reputation of being a spiritual experience, as though its sufferers simply wasted away ethereally. It was dreaded, but somehow romanticised by those whose families had not been touched by the disease. In reality, it was a long slow death for the sufferer and heart-breaking for loved ones to watch. Day after day, night after night, in cramped quarters, Jane coughed up blood-tinged sputum and sweated till the bed sheets were wringing wet. There was nothing romantic about tuberculosis.

On that last night as Mary sat by her daughter's bedside, Jane, though emaciated and weak, managed to look at her mother with a lasting intensity, unable to speak. It was as though she was trying to give her last bit of strength to her mother, before she faded away.

With her mother and brothers by her side, on May 2, 1890, aged just 22, Jane Percy McMurdo died at the family home at Barrhill Rd after suffering for nearly two years with tuberculosis.

The family burial plot in Muirkirk cemetery was becoming crowded and Mary spent more and more time by the graves of her husband and four children. She cut a lonely figure as she moved through the headstones dressed from head to toe in black, her lined face devoid of emotion. As she sat by the freshly dug earth under which her daughter's coffin had been placed, she looked around at the headstones in the kirkyard – some ostentatious and reaching for heaven and others more modest in size. Her family deserved a headstone, she thought, 'something to show the world that they once walked among the living'. She vowed to save every spare penny to pay for the headstone, and the project gave her a renewed sense of purpose.

Chapter 29 (1890)

FIRE IN THE BELLY AND
COLD COMFORT

The household now consisted of Mary and her sons Thomas, 24, a coal miner, Douglas, 17, a baker, and scholars Andrew, 11 and William, 7.

Mary battled on to care for her younger sons with the financial help of older sons, Thomas and Douglas. Neighbour and friend Keir Hardie offered the McMurdos moral support and mentored Thomas in his aspirations to further the claims of his fellow miners. Hardie had for some time been advocating that the working class needed its own political party and Thomas agreed with him. He was fascinated by this man who had started his early teenage years as an uneducated child miner, yet had developed into a cultured man with big ambitions. Thomas admired the way that Hardie made people stop and listen. He knew that Hardie was a man who was going places, who could make a difference for the working man, and Thomas was happy to walk along beside him. Thomas and his friends attended meetings that Hardie organised to get the men on side and to help form a political party. The men listened to Hardie because he was one of their own.

"The issues are plain and pressing enough for all to see," Hardie began one night at a meeting of coal miners in Cumnock. "We all live with inadequate housing, long hours underground and little provision given for our safety or our health. There are inadequate safeguards to secure that the coal you have hewed and sent up to the surface will be justly and fairly weighed and credited to you," he said as they shouted agreement. "For facing life under these conditions the money reward is completely inadequate yet the mine owner who exploits the minerals and the merchants who market the coal in this very profitable industry make no excuses for the pittance you are paid!," he said as he raised his voice and stamped the table with his fist. The men were fired up.

"As the coal market expands and the need for workers grows we must remove these injustices, and make the work more safe, reduce the hours of labour, see that a man's output is fairly credited to him and make the monetary reward more adequate," he concluded as the meeting room erupted with men raising their fists in the air and shouting. Hardie was their hero. He was an eloquent speaker and he knew what he was talking about and the Ayrshire coal miners felt they had found a kindred spirit to represent their grievances to the mine owners.

Thomas's work at the pit and his activities shoring up Hardie's political aspirations kept him busy and away from home. He couldn't bear to see his mother Mary in such pain. Every week he handed over his pay packet to her but he knew there was little that he could do to comfort her. Dougie was the more sensitive of the two brothers and it was left to him to provide a shoulder to cry on when Mary felt the need. But she was a stoic woman, made even more so by each tragedy that befell her. They all missed their father and siblings, but they dealt with their pain in different ways. Mary's always upright posture now became rigid and a smile rarely crossed her face. She made herself unavailable emotionally to her remaining children and the household felt the strain.

Christmas 1890 was a sad affair in the McMurdo household. The little house at Barrhill Rd remained cold and unadorned and Christmas passed with the minimum of fuss. Mary and her sons attended church on Christmas Day as though it were any other day, and returned to a meagre meal far removed from the Christmas dinners of years gone by. Dougie brought home some sweet buns and a Christmas pudding, compliments of his employer, but that was the extent of the Christmas cheer and they were all glad when it was over. They all had coughs and colds and were generally miserable. The little house, though too small for five people, seemed empty and cold.

Chapter 30 (1891)

THE FIGHT IS OVER

The snow fell heavily on the new year and Mary struggled physically and spiritually to keep the household together. She didn't hope for the best any more. She always expected the worst. She noticed that her eldest son Thomas's health had started to decline. He was having trouble breathing and was prone to coughing fits, especially in the mornings and when he returned from his shifts at the mines. Over the course of January, Thomas's coughing became worse and he was spitting up blood. As he tried to sleep, Mary sat in a chair in the corner of the room staring at him. She'd watched her husband George suffer with Miner's Lung contracted over many years down the mines. Surely, at just 25 and only 10 years working down below, her son Thomas couldn't have the same affliction. And Janie, how she'd coughed and fought for breath in the last stages of tuberculosis. Could that be what her son had contracted?

"This was not how it was supposed to be," Mary confided to her neighbour Keir Hardie. "Thomas has always been so full of spirit, and he's so young. He has a chance to make something of his life, and under your guidance, to do good for his fellow workers. And God knows I need him here." She placed her hand on Hardie's arm as he sat at her kitchen table. "Mr Hardie, the sooner you can do something for the men working in the coal mines of Ayrshire, maybe the whole of Scotland, then the sooner you will relieve the pain and burden of many a wife and mother who struggles through this life in fear of illness, injury, death, starvation and homelessness." Hardie placed his hand over

Mary's and tried to reassure her. "Mrs McMurdo," he began softly, "the only way the conditions of these men will improve is if they have a voice. I am that voice. Thomas is that voice. Future generations of coal miners will be the better for men like young Thomas McMurdo taking a stand. Your son is a courageous young man. You can be proud of him."

"Oh, I'm proud of all my children, Mr Hardie," Mary said. "But pride cannot save them from the life they've been given." She removed her hand from under Keir Hardie's hand, pushed both hands against the table, stood up and walked over to the fire where she stood arms folded staring into the flames. Hardie took his cue to leave and quietly closed the door behind him.

Thomas continued to go to work in the mines, but he came home from each shift weak and exhausted. Eventually, he did not have the strength to get out of bed.

In early February after a severe coughing fit, Thomas began to cough up blood more regularly and his nose started bleeding. His lungs were filling up with fluid that he could not expel. For ten days he struggled to cling to life. He tried to speak to his mother Mary but he did not have the strength. She squeezed his hand, cooled his fevered brow and tried to make him comfortable. His friend and neighbour Keir Hardie was a regular visitor to Thomas's sickbed and he sat with the ill young man some nights so that Mary could get some rest. At two o'clock on the cold, dark morning of February 26, 25-year-old Thomas McMurdo suffered a pulmonary haemorrhage and died at the little house at Barrhill Rd, Cumnock, with his friend and mentor Hardie by his side. At first light Hardie sent for Dr Kerr and gently roused Mary from her slumber. Hardie had faced angry mobs of robust men and debated with hardened politicians and lawmakers but telling this tough, yet fragile woman that she had lost another child was a chore he would gladly have foregone. Without expression, Mary walked to her dead son's bed and knelt beside him. She gently brushed his hair from his face with her care-worn hand, and kissed him on the forehead.

"Be at peace now my son," she said. "You have plenty of company waiting for you. Oh how I envy you." Then she stood up and walked outside, her thin nightgown clinging to her slender frame as the snow continued to fall. She walked directionless as Hardie watched from the door of the house. He sighed, looked back at his dead friend and walked on after Mary, gently steering her back towards his own house to the care of his wife Lillie while he returned to speak with the doctor and make arrangements for Thomas's burial. Douglas, Andrew and William sat staring into space as he returned to the McMurdo house and Hardie, the great orator, wished he had the words that would bring comfort to this family who had already endured so much, but there were no words. The contribution he could make was practical – ensuring that the Miner's Union paid for Thomas's funeral and helping Mary to find new accommodation. Now that there was no longer a miner living in the house, the mine owners would expect the family to move. Hardie wondered how they would cope with just Dougie's small wage from the bakery, but there was little more that he could do. Mary was once again having to pick up the pieces and move on.

Chapter 31 (1891)

MOVING AWAY FROM THE MINES

One thing was certain for Mary. The McMurdo family was done with the pits. She wanted better opportunities for her remaining sons Douglas, 17, Andrew 12 and William 8.

Tuberculosis was still rife throughout Scotland and the cities of Edinburgh and Glasgow had lost thousands of people over the past few years due to the disease. The medical profession was just beginning to understand that overcrowding in city slums, a lack of sanitation and poor hygiene habits were helping to spread the disease. Mary had developed a 'nothing to lose' attitude. Her family had already been devastated by tuberculosis and other respiratory diseases and she wasn't afraid. The disease was very present in the cities, but it was in Edinburgh and Glasgow where there were work opportunities and she was determined to move her family closer to a city and away from the miners' rows. She had no real choice. With no miner in the family the mine owners wanted her out of the house at Barrhill Rd, Cumnock and she needed a plan.

Douglas was now the sole breadwinner in the family – literally. He had started an apprenticeship at a bakery in Cumnock and she hoped that he could transfer to a baker in the city. Large scale industrial flour mills owned by the Incorporation of Glasgow Bakers supplied the many local bakeries in Hamilton, in the parish of Govan, and surrounding areas just outside of Glasgow. Mary thought that moving to a town of the same name as her own maiden name might be a good omen so the McMurdo family packed up their meagre possessions and boarded a train.

They travelled from Cumnock station, through Smallburn where Mary's first son Thomas had been born, on to Muirkirk where baby Andrew and the first wee Margaret died, then on to new territory as the train wound its way to a new life in the cold, grey, town of Hamilton.

Mary and her three sons settled into a small, two-roomed house on the ground floor of a tenement building. The house had some years before been leased by the greengrocer David Rodgers while the next door property had been leased by the flesher (as butchers were called) Andrew Smart. The street was a busy commercial area where merchants lived above their shops, but the increased need for housing had seen the buildings converted into one up, one down houses. Hamilton was close to the Blantyre coal fields but as far as Mary was concerned, the mining villages were a world away. There were work opportunities for her sons closer to Glasgow. At the moment she barely had enough money to put food on the table.

Next door to their little house at 25 Almada Street, Hamilton lived the Brownlies at number 27. The couple, Thomas and Agnes, had been married for eight years and had four children – Thomas 7, Mary 5, Jeanie 3 and baby James 1. Thomas Brownlie, 37, was 10 years his wife's senior. He was a Master Baker and he gladly took young Douglas under his wing so that he could complete his baker's trade apprenticeship. Mary saw this as a stroke of good luck and hoped that, with the move to Hamilton, their bad fortune was behind them.

Thomas Brownlie worked long hours in the bakery to provide for his family. Thomas was the illegitimate son of Mary Brownlie, the daughter of a Sheriff Officer. She had been shunned by the village when she was pregnant with him, because she was not married. Agnes's father James Harker was a blacksmith and he and his wife Jeanie were glad that their daughter had married a man of trade.

The McMurdos and the Brownlies got to know each other well, especially as Douglas, 17, was now apprenticed to Thomas Brownlie. The younger boys Andrew 12, and William, 8, were enrolled at the local school and Mary set about making a home for herself and her sons at their new address. The sights and sounds of the new neighbourhood were different. The coal dust hanging in the air over the miners' rows was replaced by the smog from the nearby city of Glasgow with its growing number of factories. The poverty of the miners' rows was nothing compared to the sights Mary saw as she walked through the streets of Glasgow – people in rags, coughing and begging – and her heart went out to them, but she needed every penny she had, and had to lift her head high and walk past the outstretched hands as she went about her business. She and her sons had a chance at a new life and she was determined to make it work for them.

Chapter 32 (1891)

THE WILD, WILD WEST

O n November 7, 1891 Colonel William Frederick Cody 'Buffalo Bill' and members of his Wild West Show attended a football match between Rangers and Queen's Park at the recently-opened Ibrox Stadium in Glasgow, where at half-time the legendary American showman was introduced to both teams. The Glasgow Cup tie resulted in a 3-0 victory for Queen's Park.

Just over a week later, on November 16, Buffalo Bill opened his show in the East End Exhibition Building in Dennistoun, Glasgow.

Andrew and William were desperate to see the show as their mother, and father, had told them of the escapades of the famous American Indian fighter. They had a special interest because two of their great-great-uncles had moved to America and had real experience of 'red indians' coming into their yards. The wild west show coming to town piqued their interest once again and they asked their mother Mary to tell the story once more.

After supper one night, as they were all gathered around the table, Mary took down the family bible and carefully pulled out a letter that was well-thumbed and yellow with age.

"This is a letter from your great-great-uncle John McMurdo to his mother and father back here in Scotland," Mary began. "John and his brother James emigrated to Canada in the 1820s and settled in Pennfield, New Brunswick where they married and both worked as millwrights."

"And were there Indians there?," enquired William anxiously.

"No, not there Will," his mother replied, and returned to her story.

"After they were established, about 20 years later in the 1840s they moved to Wisconsin, in the United States of America and settled in Hortonville, Outagamie County. They were some of the first white settlers in the area."

"But there were Indians there, right mither?, William insisted.

"Aye Will, there were Indians there."

William and Andrew's eyes shone brightly as they looked at their mother. Mary looked over at Douglas who was quietly smiling to himself at his brothers' excitement. Mary opened the letter that John McMurdo had written to his mother and father many years before, and began to read.

"Today we had visitors in our back yard. James and I have our mill set up on the property and plenty of wide, open space for all our tools and outhouses. This morning, just at dawn, a group of Indians came into our yard to sharpen their tomahawks on our grindstone."

"Oh!," exclaimed William as he took in a sharp breath. "Indians! In their back yard!"

"I think they're aw deed," added Andrew.

"They couldnae be aw deed else who would write the letter?," countered William as his eyes rolled in his head. "Will ye go on please mither," he said as he sat with his head propped up on his hands, elbows firmly fixed to the table.

"Well," continued Mary, "I believe they all lived to tell the tale. In fact your uncle John and his wife had a daughter who was the first white child born in the county. And they got on fine with the Indians and all lived happily together," she said and closed the letter and put it back in the bible.

"Aye, but ooh it must have been frightenin' to see, do you not think Dougie?," asked William of his eldest brother.

"Aye, it would have been terrifying Will. Would you be terrified if you saw a red Indian?," asked Douglas.

"No," scoffed William. "I'd stand there and stare at them and never move an inch," he said as he removed his hands from under his chin and stared into the eyes of Douglas who could barely contain the laughter that was building in his throat. "I'd no let them in this hoose and I'd look after mither to make sure they didn't cut her pretty hair," and he grew more serious with each new fact.

"Well, that's very good to hear our Will," teased Douglas as he reached into his pocket. "For I have here a chance for you to stare down an Indian."

William gulped and looked at his brother Andrew who was sitting wide-eyed.

Taking his hand from his pocket, Douglas continued, speaking slowly. "I have here three tickets to go to the East End Exhibition Building on Saturday night to see," he paused, then his voice grew louder, "the wild west show with real cowboys and Indians!"

Andrew and William jumped up from the table and took the tickets from Douglas, staring at them in disbelief. What a treat.

Mary shifted uncomfortably in her chair and before she could say anything, Douglas continued speaking to the boys but looking at his mother. "Some people from the show came by the bakery today and offered us some free tickets if we'd tell all our friends about the show, so it'll no cost us a penny!"

Mary sighed quietly in relief that there was no cost involved and took a moment to enjoy the excitement of her sons. They were all happy and healthy and she thanked God for them, every day.

The younger boys could scarcely sleep that night and, as the show's promoters knew, they went to school the next day and told all their friends about the wild west show they were going to see. Every boy at the school was envious and wanted a ticket and for a few days at least, Andrew and William felt special.

All day Saturday they did their chores as fast as they could and waited impatiently for Douglas to come home from work to take them to the show. He arrived, as always, with bread and buns in hand, and after supper they were off to the East End.

The boys sat enthral as the blonde, pig-tailed cowgirl Annie Oakley dressed in buckskins and broad-brimmed hat showed off her sharp shooting skills. The spectacle of dozens of American

Indians bedecked in feathers and paint and coloured blankets, sitting astride horses of every colour and shouting chants was exciting stuff for any young boy, and Andrew and William loved every minute of it. And when the indians 'attacked' a stage coach the boys eyes were bulging, then they heaved a sigh of relief when Buffalo Bill rode in to the rescue. It was a glorious night of amusement and excitement that they would never forget.

Buffalo Bill's Wild West Show had great success in Glasgow, enjoying big crowds over the four months they stayed in the city. When that fact was mentioned in the newspaper, Andrew and William liked to believe that they had played some small part in spreading the word about the show and helping to make it a success.

Chapter 33 (1892)

FOLLOWING HARDIE'S RISE

K eir Hardie had kept in touch with the McMurdo family after they moved from Barhill Road Cumnock to Almada Street Hamilton and they had watched his career blossom. His efforts on the part of all coal miners to improve their pay and conditions were indefatigable. To the Ayrshire miners particularly, he was a hero, as he was 'one of ours'. On July 4, 1892 Hardie became the first Socialist to win a seat at Westminster when he took the Essex constituency of West Ham from the sitting Conservative member in the General Election. Six months later, on January 13, 1893 the founder of the Scottish Labour Party, James Keir Hardie, formed the Independent British Labour Party.

As a speaker, Hardie didn't hold back in an attempt to drive home his point. He travelled widely to gain knowledge and present his point of view, including his strong belief in the receptive powers of the working class mind. Even when addressing an audience of workmen he did not hesitate to illustrate his point with a metaphor from science, or amplify it with a sonnet. But for all his self-education and status, he never forgot his roots and that was his appeal.

Mary read in the newspapers of Hardie's exploits and wished him well in his fight for the miners. But it was a passing interest in a former neighbour and dear friend, not the interest of someone who had a direct stake in the success of Hardie's endeavours for the miners. After all, her family was finished with that life.

Chapter 34 (1895)

THE GRIM REAPER STRIKES TWICE

B y the start of 1895, Douglas, now aged 22, had qualified as a baker and continued to work alongside his friend and neighbour Thomas Brownlie. The McMurdo family had managed to stay reasonably healthy, despite the damp and smoggy conditions in Hamilton.

Andrew, now aged 16, was working beside his brother Douglas and their neighbour Thomas Brownlie as a Baker Journeyman, learning the bakery trade. Thomas Brownlie was glad of the help as his health had taken a turn for the worse in recent months. He had started to show signs of tuberculosis some months earlier, and had no choice but to keep on working. He needed the money for his family, and the town needed bread. Thomas Brownlie's wife Agnes had given birth to another daughter, also named Agnes, so he now had five children to feed. There were times when he could not work a full day and the McMurdo boys, Douglas and Andrew, did much of the day-to-day running of the bakery, and were glad to do it. The Brownlies had been good friends to the McMurdos since their move from the miners' rows four years earlier and they were reliable, hard-working lads who could be trusted to look after things as Thomas Brownlie's condition worsened.

Towards the end of January, Thomas Brownlie could barely make it to work at all, and by the beginning of February he was confined to his bed, in the last stages of tuberculosis. Mary knew the signs – she had seen it in her own children – and helped Agnes Brownlie where she could, tending to the children while Agnes cared for her husband. Seeing Thomas Brownlie's suffering and the exhaustion in his wife brought back painful memories to Mary as she had cared for her husband and children during their last days on earth. She did what she could to keep the Brownlie children occupied but her own strength was sapped and she had little emotion to give. She rarely laughed these days, and having disease almost on her doorstep again plunged her deeper into herself.

On February 22, 1895, aged just 41, Thomas Brownlie died at 27 Almada Street, Hamilton. Agnes Brownlie, just 31, was left alone to raise five small children.

With barely enough from Douglas and Andrew's wages from the bakery to keep their own family going, the McMurdos now took responsibility for Agnes and her children, with the help of Agnes' parents James and Jeanie Harker. Somehow they managed to eke out an existence and keep the Brownlie children in school, albeit in threadbare clothes and with no shoes. Mary admired Agnes for the strength she had shown after her husband's death. It reminded her of herself and she did all that she could to help the young widow. Had it not been for Mary's mother-in-law Margaret Stevenson McMurdo's strength, love and caring, she often wondered if she would have made it this far.

Granny Margaret herself was now not well. She had been well cared for by her children and their families, with barely a minute spent on her own since her beloved Thomas had died in the Ayr River 13 years before, but her body was worn out and her appetite had waned. Mary visited her as often as she could in New Cumnock, but Margaret had taken to having 'turns' with chest pain and fainting, and rarely set foot outside these days. When Mary visited, on the odd day that there was sunshine, she would sit Granny Margaret out in the sun to thaw her old bones and get some colour into her cheeks. They enjoyed their chats together and Mary knew that, of all Margaret's daughters-in-law, she held a special place in Margaret's heart. Perhaps it was the losses they had both experienced, and the same no-nonsense approach to life, that had brought them closer together.

"Oh we had some times did we no' Mary?," Granny Margaret said on one of Mary's visits. "I remember the first time our Geordy brought you hame to meet us. Christmas it was. And your mither!," Granny Margaret laughed. "How shocked she seemed to find hersel' in a two-roomed miner's house surrounded by children." Mary laughed with her at the memory of her dear mother being overwhelmed by the noise of all the McMurdo children in the tiny house. Margaret's mood grew sombre and she reached for Mary's hand. "You were a grand wife to our Geordy, Mary, a grand wife. And the way you've handled life's tragedies, I've nothin' but admiration for ye, m' dear. Geordy knew you were a strong lass – he said so – and you are. Stay strong, dear girl."

That was one of the last conversations that Mary had with Granny Margaret.

Late in July, 1895 Mary received word that her mother-in-law had been admitted to hospital. She was lethargic and had contracted a virus that caused diarrhoea. Granny Margaret's family took turns to sit with her, and her youngest born son Andrew's face was the last she saw on earth. Shortly after he arrived for his visit, Margaret Stevenson McMurdo died from heart weakness at 7pm on July 23, 1895 at Smithfield College. Her remaining children – Thomas, 53, William, 50, James, 46, John, 43, Lizzie, 41, Rab, 39, Mary, 34, Margaret, 33 and Andrew, 32 – and their families gathered at Lizzie's house in New Cumnock for a celebration of their parents' lives. Her elder brother Thomas spoke lovingly of the times they had had together.

"I would ask ye all to raise yer glasses to Margaret Stevenson and Thomas McMurdo," he said as he held out his glass of whisky. "When our faither drowned 13 years ago in the Ayr River, it came as an awful shock to our mither and sadly she cannae lay beside him in the kirk yard. Faither liked a drink and mither never did, but she wouldnae mind us havin' a drink fer them now. Here's to a woman who raised 11 children in a house full of love, and to a man whose kindness and generosity was known throughout the village. May they now be together, with our brothers George and Davey." As Thomas finished speaking and drained his glass, his sisters wiped the tears from their eyes and hugged their children. They were descended from hard-working stock and all of Thomas and Margaret's children, without exception, were still earning a living from below the surface of the earth – their sons coal miners themselves and their daughters married to coal miners.

Margaret Stevenson McMurdo was buried in Muirkirk New Cemetery with some of her children.

Chapter 35 (1896)

LOVE BORN OF DUTY

D ouglas McMurdo had grown into a gentle, thoughtful
man running the bakery after Thomas Brownlie's death,
helping his younger brother Andrew with his bakery
apprenticeship, ensuring his mother Mary had enough money to
put decent food on the table and sharing his mother's vision that
his youngest brother William should stay at school as long as
possible.

Douglas had also grown very fond of his next door neighbour -
Thomas Brownlie's widow, Agnes. When he was not at the
bakery, or helping his mother with any jobs that needed doing,
he was next door helping Agnes and her five small children.
'Uncle Dougie' was very popular with the Brownlie children as
he brought them sweet buns most evenings, just as their father
had done.

Just as Agnes's husband Thomas Brownlie had been ten years
older than Agnes, Douglas was 10 years younger than her but the
age difference didn't stop a blossoming romance – hardly
passionate, but more a respectful relationship born from need
and empathy. Mary could see that her eldest son was smitten
with the young widow, and she watched them together on the
many evenings that Agnes and her children shared the McMurdo
tea table.

Life for Agnes and the children was not easy with no man in
the house, even with Mary and Douglas's help.

In the Autumn of 1896, Douglas waited for his brothers to
finish their evening meal and then head out the door to visit their

137

friends. He took the opportunity of some quiet time with his mother to ask her advice.

"Will ye sit doon by the fire, mither," Douglas said as he motioned his mother towards one of the fireside chairs that they had carted from house to house, and he sat down in the chair beside her.

"There's something I've been pondering on for some weeks, mither, and I'd like to know your thoughts."

Mary had an idea of the subject of the conversation but let her son do the talking.

When she was seated, he continued. "You know we are doing well down at the bakery, and things are much better here now with Andrew bringing in a wage also." He cleared his throat and continued. "You may also know that I've grown very fond of Agnes and the children." He paused and scanned his mother's face for a reaction but he got none. The pace of his conversation quickened as he continued. "Well, ye see it's like this mither. I've been thinking. It would be far cheaper to run one household than trying to run two as I'm doing now. The rent's no cheap and the children need clothes and shoes and, well, I just cannae find any other way for it."

Mary reached across the gulf between the two chairs and took her son's hand. "What is it you are trying to say, my son?," she asked.

Douglas gently released her grip on his hand, stood up and moved to lean on the mantelpiece by the fireplace, one hand in his pocket.

"I think it would be best for everyone that I marry Agnes and she and the children move in here with us so that the money will go further," he blurted out, his face turning red.

Mary was silent, her face emotionless. She had guessed that Douglas was keen on Agnes, but she was a bit taken aback that he was thinking of marriage.

"It's a lot to take on five children, Dougie," his mother cautioned. "You're just a young man yourself. Are you sure this is the right thing for you?"

"Aye mither," Douglas replied confidently. "I've given the matter a lot of thought and there's nothing else for it. Agnes is a handsome woman and has plenty of child-bearing years left in her. We can have our own children."

A faint smile flickered across Mary's face. 'A grandchild,' she mused.

"I can see the wisdom of your thinking Douglas," Mary said. "It will mean some changes for all of us, but you have my blessing son. Does Agnes know of your plans?"

"No, and I think she'll be surprised but happy. I'm away to talk to her tonight."

When Douglas made his matter-of-fact proposal to Agnes she was relieved.

"Oh Dougie," she said as she gently touched the bristles of his beard. "You know I need you and I do have a real affection for you." She paused. "It's a lot to take on a woman and five children."

Douglas rolled his eyes and placed his hands on Agnes's shoulders. "Och, I've just had this conversation with my mither," he said. "Is it to be yes or no Agnes?," he asked in his quiet way.

"I'd be honoured to be Mrs Douglas McMurdo," she said and placed a soft kiss upon his cheek.

Douglas went home with a smile on his face. He was to be married and perhaps have his own children. He could give his mother a grandchild to brighten her heart. Life was good and he was happy.

On February 23, 1897, exactly two years and one day after Thomas Brownlie's death, Douglas Percy McMurdo married Agnes Harker Brownlie. There was no celebration, and they displayed little affection in public but they were both happy with the union.

Chapter 36 (1897)

A NEW FAMILY

M ary set about rearranging the meagre furniture at 25 Almada Street and Agnes and her five children moved into the McMurdo household.

Mary gave up the double bed to Douglas and Agnes and joined her sons Andrew, 18, and William, 16, in box beds in the kitchen, where the boys hung a hessian curtain on a string to give her some privacy. Also in the kitchen, space was made for Agnes's sons Thomas and James, and the girls Mary, Jeanie and Agnes slept in another box bed in the main bedroom with their mother and new stepfather.

During the day Mary and her neighbour-now-daughter-in-law worked side by side to wash and cook for the family, but with 10 people in the household it was crowded. At night, Agnes fussed over Douglas when he came home from work at the bakery and Mary grew fond of her five step-grandchildren. It was nice to have weans in the house again and with no grandchildren of her own, Mary took them to her heart while dosing out liberal amounts of discipline when she felt it was needed. She had always been a strict disciplinarian and good manners were a must.

Within weeks of their marriage, Agnes was pregnant with Douglas's child. Douglas was thrilled at the news and not daunted in the least to have another mouth to feed. While a stout woman, Agnes was not hardy. She struggled to maintain any vitality as the pregnancy progressed. And then it began - the coughing and the night sweats. As the life within her grew stronger, Agnes grew weaker. Mary took over the primary role of caring for Agnes's children while Douglas doted on his new wife and sat up with her many a night as the hacking cough wracked her body. Her belly grew but her limbs became emaciated and in the final weeks of pregnancy she could scarcely lift her head from the pillow.

Mary knew. In her heart she knew. She could cope. She had to. But what about Douglas? Did he realise how sick Agnes really was? Mary didn't need a doctor to tell her what was wrong with her daughter-in-law, and when the doctor was called, he only confirmed her suspicions.

"It's tuberculosis," Dr Livingstone told Douglas quietly. "That, coupled with the pregnancy is taking a toll on her. At this stage the baby's heartbeat is strong, but Agnes has no strength. She needs plenty of rest if we are to deliver this baby."

The news was grim. Douglas was a gentle, sweet and loving man not given to outbursts, but he slumped in a chair by the fire, where Agnes could not see him, and wept. His mother Mary walked towards him and put a comforting hand on his shoulder.

"You'll have to be strong for Agnes and the wean," she said gently. "Show her how much you love her and reassure her that all will be well with the wean. There's no need to tell her of her fate."

Douglas hung his head in his hands and sobbed. Married not one year and already his Agnes would be taken from him. Life did not seem fair – but he already knew that.

Chapter 37 (1897)

A BRIEF MOMENT OF HAPPINESS

As the last days of Autumn gave way to cold Winter winds, Agnes's time was drawing near. She laboured throughout the night and on November 16, 1897 at 9.45am George Percy Hamilton McMurdo was born at 25 Almada St, Hamilton. Only a mother's love could push through the pain of her own disease and the agony of childbirth to ensure that her child was born safe and well. After the delivery, Agnes slept for two days but she never recovered her strength.

Despite Agnes's pain, and the heartache she saw in her son Douglas, Mary allowed herself a smile when holding her first grandchild. She fought hard to contain her joy, but she loved her grandson George and immediately took over the role of mothering the baby. She had to, as Agnes was not capable of the task. There was no mother's milk in her sick body and Mary bottle fed the baby with a formula recommended by the doctor.

She made Christmas as happy a time for Agnes's five children as she possibly could. Douglas cut down a large fir tree which the children excitedly decorated with paper chains and bits of coloured paper. It took up most of the precious space in the kitchen, but Mary didn't mind. She knew that it was the first and last Christmas that Douglas and Agnes would spend together as husband and wife, and new parents, and she wanted to give them as much time together as she could. She tended to the other children and made sure they had sweeties in their stockings on Christmas morning and that she took them to church with her every Sunday.

All Christmas Day, Douglas, Agnes and baby George stayed close together in bed. Andrew and William played with the other children to keep them occupied. Outside the snow was falling and to those who did not know, it looked like a scene of perfect family harmony. Mary was glad to be busy again. Her son and grandson needed her and after years of grieving for the loss of her husband and children, she found a reserve of strength to keep going.

Chapter 38 (1898)

THE MOTHERLESS CHILDREN

A new year dawned, but it was not a year full of promise and hope. The McMurdo family all knew that.

With the new baby in the house, Mary was even more conscious of hygiene and cleanliness. She had learned from experience what was needed for Agnes as she suffered the debilitating effects of tuberculosis. A special cup was kept for the purpose of spitting into. The doctor had given her a disinfecting solution to place into the cup to burn all contents. He also advised against kissing the infected person on the lips as people came to realise that the disease was contagious. They were not 'a consumptive family' in the sense that they were cursed with disease, but rather the medical profession and the community generally were starting to realise that the disease could be spread by coughing and sneezing. But the house was full to brim and isolating Agnes was difficult. Gradually she lost interest in trying to care for the children as the strength drained from her already fragile body. She wanted to hold her baby son and cuddle her older children but she didn't want to risk passing on the disease to them, now that she knew that it was contagious.

A month after Christmas, Agnes took her last gasping breath, as the tuberculosis filled her lungs with fluid. On January 28, 1898, at 10 minutes after midnight, Agnes Harker Brownlie McMurdo, aged just 34, died at 25 Almada St, Hamilton. Her baby son George was just two months old and her husband, at just 24, was a widower.

A month after organising his son's christening, Douglas was at the church making arrangements for his wife's funeral. Their time together had been short but it was meant to be, as their union had produced a son – proof that they had shared, if not a deep love, then a true affection for each other. Douglas had a son to carry on the family name.

After the funeral, Agnes's parents James and Jeanie Harker went back to the McMurdo household to discuss the future of their grandchildren.

"Of course, we'll be takin' the weans to live wi' us," Jeanie Harker told Mary matter-of-factly. "Thomas is old enough at 14 to help his grandfather with the blacksmithing and I could use the help around the hoose from Mary and Jeanie. And James and Agnes, well they'll be at the school."

Mary loved her step-grandchildren but she could see no other solution. Without another woman in the house, she couldn't look after them and a tiny baby.

"I know it's the best thing for them," Mary said without argument. "But I will miss them."

"Aye, but you can see them, as we'll want to see our new grandson George," Mrs Harker said.

Over a cup of tea the future of the children was settled. Mary gathered up their few belongings and gave them to Mr Harker to put on the cart. She got the children together as Douglas was still too distraught to speak.

"Now children," she said in a commanding voice. "Your grandparents will be looking after you from now on, but you can come back often to see us." Noticing the long faces of the children to whom she had been a mother figure for over a year, Mary tried to lighten the mood.

"After all, you'll be wanting to see how your wee brother George is growing. Now on you go, and mind your granny and grandpa," Mary said with a wave of her hand.

And with that, they were in the cart, five sad little faces waving goodbye to the street and the friends they had known for most of their lives, heading for a house somewhere in Lanarkshire that they'd never been.

As the clip-clopping of the horses' hooves grew ever fainter, Mary walked inside the house to see Douglas cradling his son, searching his face for traces of Agnes.

"I think he has Agnes's chin," Douglas said to Mary.

Without uttering a word, Mary warmed a bottle of milk for the baby and handed it to Douglas. The sight of her newly-bereaved son holding his infant son tugged at her heart and brought a tear to her eye. Would the sadness never end?

After Agnes's passing and the children moving in with their maternal grandparents, the house at 25 Almada Street was strangely quiet. Douglas and Andrew continued to work at the bakery and William was in his last year of schooling.

Mary, at 52, had the responsibilities of a new mother again but far from seeing it as a chore, she relished the chance to raise another child – her only grandchild. Young George thrived under her care but she was glad when his father Douglas came home from work at night to help share the load of looking after the infant. There were few fathers who helped out so much in caring for their children, but Douglas knew that Mary couldn't do it all on her own. Why should she? She had raised her own children, lost her own children, nursed Agnes when she was ill and helped him pick up the pieces of his life after Agnes passed away. He loved his mother dearly and it hurt him that she was so exhausted at night after caring for his baby, so anything he could do to help lift the burden, he would do.

Chapter 39 (1898)

TIME TO MOVE...AGAIN

A bakery apprenticeship took seven years to complete and Andrew was still apprenticed to his brother Douglas, who was now a Master Baker. Andrew's days consisted of measuring, weighing, sifting and mixing baking ingredients according to the established recipes of the bakery and introduced yeast, shortening, oil or leavening agents. He prepared bread, rolls, cakes and batters for the senior bakers and looked forward to the day when he would be finished his apprenticeship and be a qualified baker like Douglas. For now, he was just happy to be working alongside his brother.

Mary couldn't have been happier that both her sons had found occupations away from the mines, and broken the long line of miners in the McMurdo family. As her youngest child William would soon be leaving school her attention turned to trying to find him suitable employment.

Her own father William Hamilton had, at the insistence of his strong, but now departed wife, retired from stone quarrying at the mines and taken a position as a Butler which he had worked in until his death. As her son William showed no interest in the bakery trade, Mary thought about getting William into service. When he finished his schooling he was taken on as a Bonded Housekeeper's Assistant at a large house in Glasgow. He was not required to live in and for this Mary was thankful as she wanted her family around her.

With all her sons gainfully employed, far from the danger of the pits, she could see a bright future for them all.

Douglas, she thought, could marry again and have more children but he had thrown himself into his work and the subject of re-marriage was never discussed.

In fact, the memory of Agnes crushed his chest each time he passed the doorstep next door where the Brownlie family had lived and where he had spent many happy hours. His own house where he lived with his son, mother and brothers, though joyous at times, was a constant reminder of the sadness he had experienced and he wanted to move to a new house.

"Mither, would you agree that I'm the man of the house," he asked Mary one night after supper.

"Aye, that you are Douglas," Mary said, surprised that he had asked such a question.

"And you'd agree that, as man of the house, it is my right to make decisions for this family?," he continued.

Mary put down her knitting needles and gave her son her full attention.

"You have that right," she replied.

Douglas dropped the authoritative demeanour and sat down by her side.

"It's this hoose and this street, mither," he began. "I cannae stand it. I see Agnes everywhere and it strikes at my heart like a knife. We've got to get out o' here. I've got to get out o' here."

"And where would we go, son?," Mary asked hesitantly.

"There's a house for rent in Govan and I've found jobs for Andrew and me at a bakery there. It will be much closer to Glasgow for William's work too. The house is a wee bit bigger than this place and all," he said eagerly, hoping to convince his mother of the advantages of moving.

Mary stared into the fire for a minute, then looked back at her son. She could see the merit in moving. The joy of a birth lingered in the house, but so did the memory of a death and she knew it was particularly hard on Douglas.

"All right then, son. It seems you've given this your best thought. I'm in favour of the move. Make the arrangements."

Douglas seemed relieved and talked to his brothers as they returned from their night out. They had no opposition, and so it was settled. The McMurdos were on the move again.

Chapter 40 (late 1898)

HAPPY DAYS ARE HERE AGAIN

Douglas found a home for the family at 11 McLellan Street, Govan. Compared with the dirt-floor, two-roomed houses of Mary's early life in the miners' rows, the new house seemed spacious. Although Govan was an industrial area with the shipping industry dependent upon coal, and a recent surge in population leading to overcrowding in some areas, the new house on the ground floor of a tenement, had three rooms – a kitchen and two rooms that could be used as bedrooms with a small area in one corner of the room at the back that could be used for bathing in a tub.

There was plenty of room for Mary to set up house for her sons Douglas now 25, Andrew 19 and William 15, and her ten-month-old grandson George. The baby slept in the main bedroom in his cradle by Mary's bed, and Douglas, Andrew and William had box beds in the other bedroom, with a tiny box room and a claw-foot bath that the family shared. What a treat to have a bath and room to move. But best of all, Mary had a wood-burning stove, not an open fireplace, for the first time in her life. They had arrived in heaven.

While their neighbours in the rows had all been mine workers living side by side, in McLellan Street they lived in a tenement and were surrounded by other bakers and confectioners, and Douglas and Andrew had plenty in common with the other bakery workers. They formed a tight, social group and Mary got to know the Nimmos, Logans and the Johnstones who all worked in various forms of the bakery business including delivering bread in a van as James Johnstone did. It was a busy neighbourhood and Mary was happy that her sons were gainfully employed and that her grandson would grow up in a town of around 90,000 people which afforded him more opportunities than the inevitability of living in a miners' row.

Douglas busied himself with his work and playing with his son in his spare time, but apart from the odd drink after work with the other bakers, he spent a lot of time alone. He liked to walk in the woods like his grandfather Thomas used to, and enjoyed the solitude. He would often find a quiet spot to sit by the River Clyde and ponder the future, for himself and for his son. He wondered how different things would have been, had Agnes lived. Would he have been blessed with more children, he wondered. He thought often of Agnes's other children and despite his best efforts to get to see the children, he'd seen them only once since they moved in with their grandparents after Agnes died. He still had hopes that his baby son George would know his half-siblings and thought often that he would just go and visit the Harkers unannounced. While he planned and dreamed, he noticed that his energy was often sapped after a day's work, but he put it down to fatigue and grief. While his love for Agnes was born more out of a desire to help her and not a burning passion, he missed her. He was a sensitive soul who kept his feelings to himself and suffered in silence. Despite his sometimes delicate constitution, Douglas had the inner strength of his mother Mary and a desire to get on in life. He worked hard to improve the standard of living for his mother, brothers and his son. Mary was aware of her eldest son's melancholy and did all that she could to cheer him up. On November 26, 1898 Mary baked a special cake to celebrate her grandson's first birthday. She invited the neighbourhood children to afternoon tea and sent a message to the Harkers for George's half-siblings to attend, but didn't receive a reply.

Baby George gurgled and smiled at all the fuss, and that made his father smile. As the baby climbed down from his grandmother's lap, he stood and wobbled on his chubby little legs, a fat finger feeling the two small teeth in his dribbly mouth. Douglas watched from a few feet away and was thrilled when

George took his first tentative step to becoming a toddler. He felt it was a sign – a step in the right direction. Here was his son growing up before his eyes, and here was Douglas steeped in despair. He needed his son and his son needed him and he told himself then and there, as he watched George fall down and pull himself up again, that he should be in the land of the living and not in the land of what could have been. Douglas's demeanour changed and Mary noticed a spring in his step once more. As a nod to his growing maturity, instead of trimming his neat beard, Douglas grew a full beard which made him look much older than his 25 years.

For the month leading up to Christmas, Douglas held back a few pennies from his wages before giving his money to Mary, as did the other boys. The family was living in a new house and everyone was hale and hearty. They had much to be thankful for and he wanted Christmas to be special.

On Christmas Day the McMurdo family celebrated with a big tree, a goose on the table and even some store-bought presents, thanks to Douglas's thriftiness and his bartering skills with the business owners next to his bakery. Mary sat pensively at the end of the day when the house was quiet, and reflected on Christmases past when hand-made toys and clothes were all the children received in their stockings. She felt a certain satisfaction that she had been able to move her family out of the mines. Although she missed the people in the miners' rows, she had no fear as her sons went off to work each morning that they may not return. That was one worry off her mind. She dozed peacefully by the fire as the flames turned to embers, the trace of a smile across her lined face.

Chapter 41 (1899)

IT DOESN'T DO TO BE HAPPY

When 1899 dawned there was a feeling of joy in the neighbourhood. Many people in Ayrshire had suffered losses to accidents and disease in the years past, and there was a sense of renewed hope as the old century burned itself out, and the new one appeared on the horizon.

The cold Winter gave way to a glorious Spring with more days of sunshine in a row than Mary could remember for a long time. The flower markets in the town were overflowing with blossoms and the warmth of the sunshine made everyone want to be out and about. The longer days of Summer sun were not enough to dry the damp out of houses after seemingly endless months of rain, but the women who were lucky enough to have windows opened them up to the Summer breezes to air their homes and try to drive out the damp.

Mary's eldest son Douglas had stepped out of his grief over the loss of his wife, and joined the land of the living again. Her youngest son William was doing well as a Bonded Housekeeper's Assistant and toddler George was oblivious to everything except whatever he could get his teeth into. Andrew, she noticed, had become withdrawn and developed a cough, but she ignored it. They were doing so well in Govan. The boys all had good jobs and George was thriving. She could say it without fear – they were happy. She refused to entertain the idea that Andrew could have anything more than a cold.

But then it started – the hacking cough at night and the blood-stained handkerchief. He began to lose weight and complained of aches and pains. By May of that year, his appearance had changed dramatically. The tell-tale translucent skin and sunken eyes, loss of weight and hacking cough all pointed to what Mary had feared for some time. Andrew had contracted tuberculosis. The realisation made her feel numb.

On a bleak Autumn morning, after the sunshine had once again deserted the west of Scotland, Mary was up and about getting the porridge ready for her sons before they went off to work. Douglas and William were readying themselves for the day's work but Andrew was still in bed.

Mary's heartbeat quickened and she felt a tightening in her chest as she looked at her son. She slowly sat herself down by his bed and placed a gentle hand on his forehead.

"I don't think I'll go to work the day, mither," Andrew said weakly. "Could you tell Dougie that I'm no' well?"

"Aye, you rest now son. Dougie will be fine. I'll bring you some water."

Douglas finished wiping his hands on a towel and moved towards his mother as she poured a glass of water from a pitcher.

"He's been very tired at work, mither, but he said it was just a cold. I've seen the signs mysel' but I refused to believe it. He's always seemed so full of life," Douglas said.

'Aye, like our Janie," Mary replied coldly. "So full of life then so full of suffering," she said as she slammed the pitcher down on the bench. "It was all too good to be true, too good to be true," Mary said angrily. "Everything was going so well, I should have known there'd be something waiting round the corner to spoil it all. My poor Andrew – he has so much to go through," she said shaking her head. Over the past few months she had almost allowed herself to be happy. That tiny window of joy had been slammed shut. She should have known better than to let her guard down, she told herself.

"I'll be here mither," said Douglas as he put a hand on his mother's shoulder. "I'll be strong for both of you."

Mary looked into her son's eyes and knew that his words were meant to comfort her, but her heart had hardened with each tragedy and she could feel no more. Nothing and no one would comfort her. She had to be stoic and get on with caring for her ailing son. No amount of talk would solve the problem.

Andrew battled on for the rest of that year, going to work when he could but staying in bed when the disease debilitated him. No one gave a thought to the fact that the town baker coughing into the dough may help spread the disease throughout the community. Many people were still not washing their hands regularly, but not in the McMurdo household. She may not have able to control what happened outside of her home, but in her house cleanliness was next to Godliness.

By New Year's Eve 1899, when Mary had hoped to be ridding herself of the pain of the past few years and welcoming in a fresh century full of hope and promise, she knew it was not to be. Instead of celebrating with their neighbours, they had a quiet new year's eve at home with tea and scones. The hours together became more precious as the life slowly drained out of Andrew.

The first day of the new century arrived – January 1, 1900 – with dancing in the street, people banging on pots and pans, and great celebration. Inside the house at 11 McLellan Street, the mood was sombre. Mary and her sons Douglas and William sat at the kitchen table. Even the warmth from the fire could not cheer them. They knew that by this time next year, their number would once again be diminished.

In the late Spring of 1900, Douglas moved Andrew's bed to beside the window where he could look out at the neighbours' gardens and see the birds fly about the trees. They did all they could to make his last days on earth comfortable but Andrew suffered the terrible rigours of the disease that they knew all too well.

Mary sent baby George next door to Mrs Logans during the day, so that she could care for Andrew. The medical profession had been warning people for some time that tuberculosis was contagious, but that didn't stop most families from caring for their sick loved ones in very confined conditions. Going to hospital was not an option as far as Mary was concerned. It was her duty to care for her children, and she did so with efficiency and the love that only a mother could bring.

On July 17, 1900 at 5.15pm the inevitable happened. Andrew Stevenson McMurdo, a Baker Journeyman, died of tuberculosis at 11 McLellan St, Govan. He was just 20 years old. Just as she had buried her first son called Andrew Stevenson McMurdo all those years before, this beloved Andrew was laid to rest in the family plot at Muirkirk.

The little family now consisted of Mary's remaining children Douglas, 26 and William 17 and her two-year-old grandson George. She was 54 years old and had seen more pain in a lifetime than anyone deserved. The sadness that settled over the McMurdo household was palpable.

Mary dragged herself through each day, but she kept herself busy so that she did not have time to sit and think. However at the end of the day she had time for nothing but thinking, as sleep eluded her. Each night as she lay down to rest, she saw the faces of her husband and the children she had lost. She spoke their names softly and pined for what might have been, had they lived. Then she would gaze across at her sleeping grandson George and wonder what lay ahead in his life. Would he be healthy and grow to have a family of his own? She hoped so, and sometimes that happy thought was enough to send her off to sleep for a few hours, before she once again found herself awake in the dark, consumed by sorrow but always with hope that a new day would be free of sadness.

Chapter 42 (1900)

NOT MUCH MORE TO GIVE

Douglas continued to enjoy his work as a Master Baker. A new bread baker, John Miller, had started work at the bakery a few months before to fill the gap left when Andrew could no longer come in to work.

John Miller was the same age as Douglas and they struck up a friendship.

"How is your mither holding up," John asked Douglas one day at work.

"Oh, she puts on a brave face, but that woman has had so much hardship in her life I can barely begin to tell you," Douglas said shaking his head as he took a tray of bread out of the oven.

"I was wondering, Douglas, if your mither could use some extra money. I'm no' pleased with the boarding house I'm staying at and, if you had room, I was wondering if she would take me in as a boarder," John said.

"Oh aye, I'm sure that'd be nay bother," Douglas said.

He asked his mother that night about taking in John Miller as a boarder. At first Mary dismissed the suggestion. She was tired and had enough to do, but the thought of more money in the household swayed her and she agreed.

John Miller moved in and shared the bedroom with William and Douglas, while young George shared the bed with Mary in her bedroom.

John was a strong, sturdy lad with dark, wavy hair and sparkling green eyes. He hailed from Stonehouse, a rural area on Avon Water near the Clyde Valley close to the town of Hamilton. He was a happy soul, and his bright spirit brought a spark back into the McMurdo household.   He was a respectful young man, and Mary like him instantly.

'He'll be a good pal for our Dougie', she thought. 'It will do him good.'

In the late Autumn of 1900, as the chilly winds summoned Winter and whipped up the fallen leaves on the street, Douglas walked home from the bakery, his coat collar turned up against his neck, cloth cap pulled down low on his face. He had grown a bushy beard two years earlier and already at age 27, his hairline was receding like his father George's had done. It was his son's third birthday and he carried in his hands a special cake that he'd made at the bakery.   He was almost home when a violent coughing fit shook his body and he struggled to hold on to the cake. He set it down beside the road, and leaned against a tree for support as he struggled for the breath that rattled in his chest. He composed himself and picked up the cake and continued on home. He always suffered from colds in the colder months, and put it down to a weak constitution, but the strain of losing his wife, the stepchildren that he had become close to, and his brother had taken a toll on Douglas and he could not shake this cold.

He reached his house, pushed open the door and safely placed the cake on the table before collapsing in another coughing fit. His mother Mary ran to fetch him a glass of water and took off his cap and coat then guided him to a seat by the fire.

The water settled the cough and he began to feel better as the warmth from the fire thawed out his bones. He rubbed at his legs to relieve the aching then sat back in the chair, sapped of strength.

Mary put the kettle on and found three candles which she lit then placed on the cake. Young George was seated at the table, eyes glued to the cake, while his Uncle William, grandmother Mary, and the boarder John Miller wished him a happy birthday, and Douglas joined in where he could between raspy breaths. They all applauded loudly and encouraged George to blow out the candles which he managed to with one breath, eliciting more applause from his gang of admirers.

As Mary went to fetch a knife, George leaned over and scooped up some delicious icing with his chubby little finger, to peals of laughter from everyone. He was doted on by them all, and as he had never known his own mother Agnes, was blissfully unaware of the gaping hole in his life.

After the remains of the cake were cleared away, Douglas, William and John sat down at the table to play cards while Mary got George off to sleep, and took her position in her chair by the fire to knit a few more rows of a vest for her grandson.

During the game, Douglas was again taken with a coughing fit. Mary remained motionless, with her back to the boys, but John looked across at William and they held each other's gaze. John had seen Douglas bent over in coughing fits at the bakery. He'd seen for weeks the way Douglas struggled to lift the baking trays and he often found his friend out the back of the bakery, sitting on the stoop, head lowered, energy drained from his body.

As Christmas 1900 brought heavy snow and rain, Douglas's conditioned worsened. He could no longer work at the bakery and John Miller offered to work extra hours to help out and to contribute more money to the household. William also asked his employer if he could take on extra work to make some more money and the family seemed to manage without Douglas's wage.

The visible skin between his receding hairline and the bushy, greying beard was pale and translucent and Douglas's thin body grew even thinner. He was troubled by aches and pains in his arms and legs and often kept John and William awake at night as he cried out in pain.

Mary became even more hard-hearted, the lines etched on her face grew deeper and her glance became cold. She kept everyone at arm's length as she robotically went about her daily chores. Douglas and William knew it was her way of coping. Each time the realisation hit her that she was going to lose one of her children, she turned to stone, withdrawing affection and scarcely speaking. She showed little emotion as Douglas's disease progressed. It was the scourge of the McMurdo family and Mary could barely bring herself to say the word – tuberculosis. How she hated that word.

Towards the end of March, Douglas knew his days on earth were drawing to a close. Mary was out doing some shopping and John was at work. William, now 17, was looking after wee George as Douglas lay in his bed. While all was quiet, Douglas called his brother to his side. He motioned to William to sit down by his side.

"Will, I think ye know where I'm headed," Douglas began softly.

"Oh Dougie, dinnae say such things," William said as he looked deeply into his brother's eyes.

"Now Will, you will soon be the man of the house and ye must be strong. I've a couple of things I must say to ye, while I can," he continued weakly.

"You're a good lad and you'll do well in life. Keep working hard and make mither proud. You're her last hope," Douglas said before pausing to cough and spit up blood into his handkerchief.

"You're to take care of mither. She'll be heartbroken all over again and she'll need you. And ye must watch over George. Promise me you'll watch over my son. Promise me," Douglas demanded urgently as he reached out his thin hand and grabbed on to his brother's arm.

"Aye, Dougie you've no cause to concern yoursel', I'll watch over George," William said.

"See that he goes to school and mind what mither tells you. She'll know what's best for my lad but she'll no' be around forever. I need to go to my rest knowing that I've entrusted the care of my son to my only brother," Douglas said as his voice trailed off.

William straightened his back and lifted his head.

"I'll take good care of the little lad, Dougie. I'll treat him like my own."

"Oh, I know you're just a lad yoursel' Will, and it's a lot of responsibility to put on yer young shoulders, but he's going to need you. And I need you now....," Douglas was exhausted and could not finish the sentence. He fell asleep, his mouth gaping open, his breathing laboured.

William pulled the blankets around Douglas's neck and walked outside into the slush that the rain had made of the remaining Winter snow. He wanted to cry, but he had to be the man of the house. He asked God to give him the strength and the guidance to do as his dying brother had asked him. 'Please God, help me look after wee George and help me comfort mither when our Dougie has gone. I don't know how much more she can take.'

Then he walked back inside, picked up his nephew from his bed, and held him high in the air. Douglas had stirred as William came back into the house and looked over at his brother and son.

"Looks like it's you and me, George. We're the men of the hoose and we'll have to take care of your gran. What do ye say laddie?"

Douglas smiled.

After talking with William, the plans for his son's future in place, Douglas grew ever weaker. Mary and William watched him suffer during his last days and prayed that it would soon be over. And it was. On April 28, 1901 at 11.30pm Douglas Percy McMurdo, Master Baker, died age 28, at 11 McLellan St Govan. His son George was now an orphan at just three years of age. Mary Hamilton McMurdo had borne eight children and buried seven of them.

Her remaining child William and her grandson George were all that were left of her family. She'd kept them out of the mines, but she couldn't shield them from the scourge of tuberculosis that had been sweeping the country. There was no more that she could have done and yet she was plagued by guilt.

In her darkest hours, alone in her bed at night, she asked herself 'why my children – why have I not contracted this despicable disease? Why am I still here?' Then she'd look across at George sleeping in his bed and her son William in the other room, and know her purpose. 'I've got to raise these boys and no one will take them from me,' she told herself.

Despite her dour demeanour, there was a fighting spirit in Mary Percy Hamilton McMurdo that even the death of her nearest and dearest could not extinguish. She lived each day with purpose and a belief that one day it would all be right. The events of the past few years would have crushed a lesser soul. Although she held her emotions in reserve, it was a mother's love that was driving her on.

Chapter 43 (1901)

A BOY BECOMES A MAN

After Douglas passed, John Miller stayed on in the household as a boarder and Mary was glad of the extra money. Young William still earned very little in service, but his employer was generous and, aware of the sadness that had engulfed the McMurdo family, often sent home game and preserves for Mary's table. She was grateful of course, but she didn't like charity and wished that things could have been different. She wished that her husband and her sons and daughters had lived, and that she was surrounded by grandchildren, but she knew she was blessed to have wee George. She was thankful that Douglas had wanted to marry Agnes and from that marriage came her treasured grandson. The little boy and her only remaining child William were the bright spots in her otherwise sad and lonely life.

In the outside world the dawning of the new century had generated hope of a better future, as the country progressed after the major changes that came with the industrial revolution. Things would become 'easier' people were told by politicians, but 'easy' was not a word Mary was familiar with. She'd always done things the hard way, it seemed to her. The work of the men and women in her family had been hard, weather and living conditions had been hard and birthing and burying children was hard. The extreme sadness of the past few years had taken their toll on Mary. She was a woman of 55, widowed, a mother to one and a grandmother to one, and housekeeper to a boarder. That was the sum total of her life and it saddened, even angered her. She had things to do – practical things like cooking and cleaning, that she had done all her life – but her body seemed to work independently of her mind and spirit. She did what she had to do, but she felt little. Her emotions were in severe shock and she felt more comfortable in the shell she had created for herself. 'Why bother engaging with anyone,' she thought. 'Relationships are brief and fleeting and I can't bear any more hurt.' She had shut herself off from neighbours and friends and spoke rarely.

William, although only 18, was mature for his age – he had to be. He had always felt as though he had been watching some sad tableau unfold around him and now he was right in the middle of it. His mother and his nephew depended on him and he had promised his brother on his deathbed to watch over young George. It was a promise that he aimed to keep. He knew that the child needed a father figure in his life and he spent a lot of time with him, taking wee George for walks in the woods just as William's father had done with him. They would throw stones in the river and young George would run around with the carefree abandon owed to any three-year-old child. The child was well cared for, William saw to that.

But it was his mother Mary who worried William the most. He had to find a way to bring her out of herself, to rejoin the living and find some joy in life again. But he knew that she was afraid to love as almost every person she had ever loved had been taken from her.

Mary spent a lot of time in her chair by the fireplace, just thinking.

She thought about how sad her mother would have been about Queen Victoria dying in January of that year, and how her husband George would not have shed a tear for an 'English' queen. Mary sympathised with Victoria. She had lived, and mourned, for 40 years without her beloved husband Albert, but at least she had her children to comfort her.

After years of saving, Mary finally had enough money to visit the stonemason and a large headstone, bearing the names of her departed husband and children, was erected in the Muirkirk Cemetery. She had the public acknowledgement that these people had walked the earth and the headstone ensured that they would not be forgotten.

Chapter 44 (1901)

BREAKING THROUGH

There was a whole world beyond the confines of 11 McLellan Street, Govan and William wanted his mother to be part of it, or at least to know about it.

Mary had always loved to read the newspaper, but even that pleasure she had abandoned. One Sunday evening, as Mary sat in front of the fireplace staring at the flames, William sat at the kitchen table and opened the new newspaper, *The Cumnock Chronicle*, which had begun publishing that year. He scanned the pages looking for some local news about the village they had once called home.

As his mother hadn't engaged in social conversation for some weeks, William turned his attention to young George who was still playing with a bowl of barley pudding long after the other dishes had been cleared.

"Let me see," William began as he looked over the pages of the broadsheet to his four–year-old nephew. "The New Cumnock Golf Club has just been designed by architect Willie Fernie. Well, isn't that something young Geordy?," William asked the child who was now painting the table with his pudding. "And you'll never guess who's got married," he continued, but it was of no use. Still Mary did not budge from her chair by the fire. No flicker of emotion crossed her face and William was at his wit's end. He couldn't continue to work all day in service and come home to see the sadness in his mother and take care of his nephew.

He put the newspaper on the table, rose from his chair and ran his hand through little George's hair and smiled at the child, as he moved to the empty chair by the fire. Sitting on the edge of his seat, he looked at his mother, who was still staring into the flames, and chose his words carefully.

"Mither," he began. "Mither, I don't believe I understand yer pain and I'll no' try to pretend to." He paused and still Mary sat motionless as a stone. "I know ye've suffered as no mother should ever suffer, but young George needs you. I need you. And I promise ye mither, I'll never leave you. Look at me," William said as he beat his hands against his chest. "Hale and hearty. You won't lose me. You won't," he urged. "Just try to love again, mither, that's all I ask," and he slumped back in the chair, exasperated. After a few minutes, Mary had still not moved and William rose from the chair to attend to George. As he passed her chair, Mary held out her hand and caught him on the arm.

"Son," she began. "It's a pain I don't know how to move past. It's an aching in my heart, in every bone in my body through to my very soul. I feel such emptiness within, I don't know what to do."

William expected his mother to cry, but she did not. She simply sat still and expressed herself the best way she knew how – in plain and simple terms, with no emotion.

"One after the other," Mary continued, "one after the other they've been taken from me, and for what? What is the reason? The church can't tell me, the doctors can't tell me, so I'm asking you my only son, why were your brothers and sisters taken from us in such a cruel way?" Mary turned in her chair and looked William in the eye.

"The truth to tell, I'm afraid to love you and wee George, for God knows everyone I love is taken away and each time the hole in my heart grows bigger. So much of my heart has been eaten away, I've nothing left to give you."

William dropped to his knees beside his mother's chair.
"That's no' true, mither," William said as he held back a tear that threatened to roll down his cheek. "Ye have love to give and love to receive." He turned his head to the left and looked at little George who sat wide-eyed and alone at the table. "You've

167

a grandson who loves and needs you. The lad's an orphan, mither. We are all he has. He loves you with all his heart and you've got to show him love as well or he'll grow up not knowing the love he's entitled to."

Mary was surprised at the wisdom with which her son spoke. She swallowed hard and pressed her hand harder into William's arm. William freed himself from her grip and moved to the table, picked up George and brought him back to Mary. He placed him in her lap and the child immediately threw his arms around his grandmother's neck and hugged her tightly. His little, smiling face beamed at her and she couldn't help but be moved by the child's innocence and pure love. William watched as Mary hugged the child and he allowed the tear to roll down his face as he stood behind her chair.

"You see, mither, you've got to take a chance on love. The wee lad and I love you – you are our world and we want you in it."

"Oh Will," Mary began. "You're so much like your dear father. He always knew just what to say in his own quiet way to cheer me up." She started to smile at little George as he wriggled on her lap. "Look at this wean," she said. "There's so much joy left in life, and I've shut myself off. And you my son," she said turning her gaze to William. "You have been so strong throughout this whole terrible time. You've seen so much pain, as I have, and now you've your gloomy old mither to deal with. But don't worry son. I'll be back to rights soon. As I've done in the past, I'll lock the sadness away in my heart."

George got down from Mary's lap and started running around the kitchen table.

"It's time this lad was in his bed," Mary said to William as she began to rise from her chair.

"Never ye mind, mither," William said as he scooped wee George up in his arms. "I'll put him in his bed. But tomorrow night, you can do it."

As William took George to his bed, Mary returned to the warmth of the fire and called over her shoulder: "You're a good son, Will," and William's heart melted. How he'd longed to hear his mother say she loved him, but it was not Mary's way to show affection. He would probably never hear the words "I love you" any time soon, but "You're a good son" was near enough.

Chapter 45 (1902)

THE FUTURE TAKES A BACKWARD STEP

In 1902 wee George started school in Govan. Mary loved the child and since her talk with her son William, she had begun to show George a mother's love, instead of a grandmother's love, for that was the position she found herself in. He was a good quiet lad, much like his father Douglas, and Mary and her son William made sure that the little lad was well turned out for class. None of the children wore shoes to school but his clothes were freshly laundered and pressed and his hair combed and neat. For Mary, life was neat and tidy, just the way she liked it. But William's job as a Bonded Housekeeper's Assistant paid very little and, even with a boarder, they were still living a meagre existence. William had the financial responsibilities for his mother and nephew and knew that one day he would want to start a family of his own. He'd thought long and hard about his prospects in his current position but just could not see how he would ever have enough money to take care of everyone on the pittance he received for his work.

As Mary was setting the table for supper one evening, she looked across at George sitting on his box bed practising his numbers and allowed a flicker of a smile to leave her mouth. William came in from his day's work and hung his cap on the peg by the door. "Hello there son, your supper will soon be on the table," she said.

"Is our boarder not in for dinner tonight, mither?," William enquired.

"No," Mary scoffed, "he's away calling on his lady friend again – three nights in a row!"

William had been trying to find a way to broach a subject with his mother and with their boarder John out of the house, this was as good a time as any.

Mary brought a big pot of rabbit stew to the table and began to dish out portions to the three plates. "Come along Geordie," she called to her grandson, "come and get yer tea."

The wee boy put down his pencil and book and scampered to the table. Mary sat across from George, and William sat at the head of the table.

"Thank you for the food, dear Lord," was Mary's regular and short blessing, before they began their meal. William took a few mouthfuls, then nervously began his speech.

"Mither, I've been thinking about the future."

"Oh aye son, it's good for you to plan ahead," Mary replied.

"Aye, so it is. And that brings me to the wages I'm earning," he paused, then hurriedly continued, "which are adequate and the work's safe, but it's just no' enough. And I've got to do something about it. Something else."

"Oh aye, and what would this something else be then?," Mary asked as she looked at her son earnestly.

"The local colliery in Cumnock is looking for miners and...". Before he could finish his sentence Mary had put down her fork and lifted her napkin to her mouth. Poverty was no excuse for lack of manners, she'd always said, and napkins on the table each night were a requisite. She sat back in her chair and stared at her son.

William tried to continue what he had to say, but Mary cut him short.

"Haven't I tried hard to keep you safe and away from the pits? Haven't I always told you not to go underground and have it kill you the way it killed your father? Have I no' told you son? Do you not understand the danger and heartache a man down the pits causes to his mother – and then the wife you'll have one day. Oh Will, you've no' thought this through. We're doing fine."

"Aye, mither, for now. But I have to think ahead. If I go to work in the mines, we'll get a house with a cheaper rent, we'll get cheaper coal for the fire and now that you have taken on the full care of wee Geordie, I can work shifts and make more money. The New Cumnock Collieries Company is expanding and looking for strong young men. Working in a big house is no' man's work. Fetching and carrying for the landed gentry. I've stood about all I can take of it. I want to do a man's work, the way my faither and grandfaither and brother did. I want to feel the sweat on my body at the end of each day and the coin in my hand at the end of each week."

"You make it sound so romantic Will, but it's not. It's hard work in cramped, hot conditions and the money is not that good."

"Aye, but it's better than what I'm earning now – and I might get some satisfaction from hard physical labour for I'm no' getting any pleasure now in the work I'm doing."

"It sounds to me as though you have made up your mind Will."

"Aye, that I have mither. I'm to start on Monday morning. I've given my notice at the big house and because I've worked out my bonded time, they have to let me go. I'm free to do as I please – and this is what I please."

Mary reached across the table and put her hand on her son's arm.

"May God go down below with you," was all she said, and resumed eating her stew.

She knew that Will was a man who could make up his own mind, and she prayed that she would not lose him to the black holes beneath the earth.

She was 56 years old with a 20-year-old son who, she believed, was making a great mistake by going to work in the mines. But he was a man and she had to trust his decision. All that she could do was wash his clothes, get his piece-box ready for working down below as she had done for his father and brother, and keep house the way she always had. She also decided that she would put a great effort into seeing that her grandson George had a good education and would not go down the mines. The wee lad would have a good future, she would see to that - a future that did not include working in the pits. Even though she had fought hard for many years to keep her sons from working in the pits, she knew she had lost the battle with William. Her last hope was young George and she would do all in her power to find him another occupation. George would not become a coal miner.

Chapter 46 (1902)

BACK IN THE FAMILY 'BUSINESS'

The village of Cumnock was thriving with a town hall, cottage hospital, public library and an athenaeum. Coal and ironstone were extensively mined in the neighbourhood. The population consisted of mainly coal and quarry workers.

Mary did not want to return to the days of living in the miners' rows, barely eking out an existence in a tiny house, and she made that clear to her son.

The McMurdo family moved to a little two-room house in the village and Mary found herself back at Barhill Road Cumnock, this time at number 48. William started work at the nearby colliery where he'd taken on a job as a coal hewer. It was dangerous work cutting coal and removing it from the coal face but it paid well and he was young and strong – and his mother didn't need to know the details.

Five-year-old George was enrolled at the Old Cumnock Public School on Barrhill Rd and Mary set about making the place a home, as she had done many times before. They did not have a lodger now, so it was just Mary in the hole in the wall bedroom, and William and young George on set-in beds in the kitchen. She no longer had the luxury of the clawfoot bath she'd had in Govan and the stove was much smaller but, it was an easy walk into the village shops and Mary quickly made friends with the other mining and quarrying families. George played in the street after school with his school friends, and life was good. There was plenty of coal for the fire, thanks to William's new job, and Mary once again had a spring in her step.

William shielded her from the realities of life working in a mine, much the way his father had done. He started off on the day shift. The hewers were divided into fore-shift and back-shift men. William's working day started at four in the morning, working through till ten. He would also take his turn at the back-shift, week about, starting at 10 and working through till four. It was his job to cut and loosen the coal from the bed. Whether the seam was so thin that he could hardly creep into it on hands and knees or whether it was thick enough for him to stand upright, it was hard and important work and a great responsibility, fraught with danger from falling coal.

Every man on the fore-shift marked '3' on his door as a sign to the caller to wake him at that hour. For the first week of his employment, he had worked with another hewer to learn the job. On his first day working alone as the fore-shift hewer, upon hearing the knock at the door, William dressed in his pit clothes which consisted of a loose jacket, vest and knee breeches, all made of thick white flannel, long stockings, strong shoes and a close-fitting thick leather cap. Many of the hewers preferred to go to work on an empty stomach, but William always packed a piece of bread and a tin bottle full of water (known as his bait), his Davy lamp and baccy-box and crept out into the darkness of the early morning without waking his mother or his nephew.

At the pit-head he got into a cage and was lowered to the bottom of the shaft where he lit his lamp and proceed 'in by' to an appointed place to meet the deputy.

"Morning young Will," said the deputy, Angus Laidlaw. "Hand me yer lamp lad," said Angus who examined and locked the lamp before declaring it safe and handed it back to William.

"On ye go, pick in one hand, lamp in the other, just like ye were telt," old Angus instructed as he patted William on the shoulder and sent him on his way.

William, eager with anticipation, strode on for about 50 yards then the roof under which he had to pass seemed to move towards him and was not more than three feet high. He kept his feet wide apart, his body bent at right angles with his hips and head well down, face turned forward as he had been instructed.

After another 300 yards he reached his destination, took off his coat and got to work.

He cut a slot in the base of the coal seam so that coal would drop, without the roof caving in. He hewed out about 15 inches of the lower part of the coal and worked up the sides then filled his first tub of coal. He continued on hewing and filling tubs until his shift was over.

Exhausted, he dragged his tired body from the depths of the mine and blinked in the mid-morning sunlight, the way his grandfather Thomas had done over 40 years before, and the way his father George and brother Thomas had done many times. As he enjoyed the gladness of having spent his first day in 'real' work, a pride washed over him as the memories of his father, brother and grandfather – proud, hard-working coal miners – came flashing back.

William walked the mile to the little house on Barhill Road, where his mother Mary was ready with warm water, soap, towel and the old tin tub that he had seen his father and brother wash up in so many times after they returned from the mines. He took the towel from his mother's hand and thought he saw a glint in her eye. Was she secretly glad to have a miner in the family again? Did it bring back memories to her of the days that she tended to his father after a shift at the mines? William took the towel and went to the lean-to out the back to wash off the honest sweat and coal dust. His chest swelled with pride. He truly felt like the man of the house, the provider who would make sure that his mother and nephew were well cared for. He had done a hard day's work – a man's work – and it felt good.

Mary placed a steaming bowl of porridge on the table and William ate hungrily.

"How was your shift, son,?" Mary asked.

"I worked hard, mither," William replied. "I think faither would be proud."

"Aye, that he would," was all that Mary said, but it was enough for William. He was back in the family 'business' and he was happy.

Chapter 47 (1911)

SHAPING UP

Life had settled into a happy pattern for Mary, her son William and grandson George. They had made good friends at Barhill Road and William had managed to escape serious injury in the pits, although there were days when he came home with gashes in his legs and arms from falling coal. But his injuries weren't serious enough to keep him away from work for more than a day or serious enough to outwardly worry his mother, although she prayed for his safety every day and was always glad to see his face at the door at the end of a shift.

There was one thing that Mary worried about more than anything. William was now 28-years-old and had never brought a girl home to meet her. One night after dinner when George had gone to bed, and Mary and William sat in the chairs by the fire, she broached the subject with him.

With needlepoint in hand, Mary casually opened up the conversation.

"How's your work, son?," she enquired.

"All very well, mither," William answered absentmindedly as he scanned the newspaper.

"I see a new family has moved in down the road. Three daughters I believe they have, all in their twenties," she continued.

"Aye, I've seen them."

"Fine lasses they are I'd say, would you not?"

"Oh aye, they're fine lasses."

"Have you had occasion to speak to any of them?"

"I've said hello as I've passed them by."

"Any one of them that you think is bonnier than the other?"

"Oh, they're all bonnie lasses, that's no lie."

William continued on answering his mother's questions as a smile crept across his face, while Mary continued on with her needlepoint and he continued to scan the newspaper.

He enjoyed the mental sport with his mother and thought he'd string her along for a while longer.

"They're names are Jenny, Ellen and Maggie," he said.

"Oh, so you've met them then," Mary said as she turned to her son and put her needlepoint in her lap.

"Not much gets past me, mither," William replied with a smile as he turned to face her.

"Oh Will," Mary said as she allowed herself a small chuckle, "don't be teasing your poor old mother."

"Have no fear, mither. I've an eye for a pretty girl and that's a fact. But I'll be finding a wife in my own time and now's not the time. She'll have to be a very special girl and I'm willing to wait."

"Aye, well don't wait for too long son," Mary replied. "I'd like some more grandchildren before I'm too old to bounce them on my knee."

"You've plenty of good years left in you yet, woman. Plenty of years," William said and they both got back to their business of needlepoint and scanning the newspaper.

George was now 13 years old and fast becoming a young man. William had raised him as his own, just as he had promised his older brother Douglas on his deathbed. The boy had always been quiet, just like his father had been, but he was a good grandson to Mary, never causing her an ounce of trouble at school or in the village, and he loved and admired William as he would his own father.

Whether it was racing hormones in his teenage body or frustration at never knowing his own parents, George's temperament had begun to change. He was moody and broody and had started getting into fights at school. The men of the pits were hard men – men who were used to defending themselves physically – and George wanted to be like them. He'd seen enough street fights and some of the lads at his school came from homes where there was either domestic abuse or the fathers and sons got into fist fights. No wonder the other lads felt confident about starting fights and picking on the smaller, younger boys.

He didn't know whether it was because he was an orphan or because he was quiet and reserved, but George had become a target for bullies at school. He knew that fighting would upset his grandmother Mary, but he was running out of excuses to give her for the bloody nose that he often came home with. He was surprised that it was his grandmother who raised the subject of self-defence.

As he walked through the door one afternoon with blood on his face and shirt, Mary took the enamel bowl down from the kitchen shelf and added warm water and disinfectant, as she always did. She set about cleaning up George's face.

"Who did this to you Geordy,?" she enquired.

"Oh, the same lads as usual, gran," George replied off-handedly.

"And do you no' fight back,?" asked his gran.

"Aye, I try to gran, but they're bigger than me and they know how to use their fists," George said indignantly.

"And do you not know how to use your fists?," his grandmother asked.

Surprised, George replied: "I thought you were against fighting, gran."

"Aye, I am, but no' when you're coming home beaten to a pulp, day after day. That's no' fighting, that's tormenting and I'll no' stand for it." She continued to clean up his wounds.

"It seems to me that we have two choices Geordy," she said. "Either I go to see the schoolmaster and the mother of these boys...,".

"Oh no, gran," Geordy cut her off mid-sentence. "Don't do that."

"Or," she continued, "you speak to your uncle William about some boxing lessons."

George looked at her in astonishment. Here was his grandmother, the women he adored and who he had tried so hard for to not get into fights, and she was telling him to learn to box.

Mary stopped blotting at his face with the cloth.

"It's one thing to go around picking fights, but it's quite another to allow yourself to be beaten up. McMurdos stand up for themselves, Geordy. Make no mistake about that. There are times when a man has to defend himself and I believe the time has come. Speak to your uncle William after supper," she said and got up from the table to dispose of the bloodied water.

George felt a surge of energy run through his wiry body and couldn't wait to talk to his uncle.

The next afternoon, when William returned from his work, George was pacing up and down outside their house, in readiness for his first boxing lesson. A group of his friends, and aggressors, had gathered too. Without saying a word, William dropped off his piece-box at the house and started to walk to the old stone bridge at the end of the road. George walked quickly to keep up with him and the growing gang of onlookers marched along behind. When they reached the bridge, William took off his coat and placed it on the ground and George did the same. William lifted his arms and clenched his fists and motioned to George to do the same.

"Keep yer heid doon and yer fists up," were the only instructions that William gave his wide-eyed nephew, then he started to spar with the boy.

"Lead with yer left and keep yer right up. Go for the gut, then right in the neb," said William as he started to dance around and George copied him. "Now try to land one, right in m' face."

George hesitated. "Come on lad," William whispered, "they're all watching you."

George danced around, leading with his left and keeping his right fist up. He took a couple of swings, but William ducked and weaved to escape any of the blows. George was embarrassed in front of the other boys and his temper flared. He landed a blow in his uncle's stomach with his left hand, and followed through with his right hand landing a blow on

William's nose. It was a superficial blow but, noticing the reaction of the other lads, William played it up for all it was worth. He reeled slightly, then clutched at the bridge for support. He put his hand to his nose and saw that George had drawn blood – it was a scratch really. William held his nose and made sure that the others could see the blood.

"I'm sorry uncle," George whispered.

"Never heed that, lad, keep dancing around wi' yer fists up," William said softly.

George kept his fists up and continued to dance around, while William groaned.

"Take another swing at me, boy," William whispered. George waiting for William to straighten up and put his fist up again, then landed another right cross on his uncle's nose.

"No more," William said, "I've had enough." He grabbed George's right arm and thrust it in the air. Then he picked up his coat and headed for home. George picked up his coat and followed his uncle. Several of the boys slapped him on the back and they all followed him home, branching off as each got to their own doors.

When George walked through the door of his house, his uncle and his gran were seated at the table waiting for him.

"That, my boy, is called the art of bluff," William said. "Ye looked confident, the others thought ye were confident and the rest was bluff. And I can almost guarantee that ye won't have any more trouble at school, because now they all think ye can fight. And that's enough."

"The McMurdo men are smart men," his grandmother said. "It's good to know that you can defend yourself if you have to, but it's much smarter to bluff yer way out of a situation. Remember that Geordy."

"Aye," said William, "but it's even better to have both – the ability to defend yoursel' physically and the ability to bluff and talk your way out of a situation. You'll learn both, I can guarantee that."

"Aye," said George, who was feeling rather pleased with himself after being hailed a hero by his friends and foe alike.

"But it's certainly a good feeling to win a fight," he said as he sat back in the chair with a satisfied look upon his face and folded his arms across his chest.

"Have you no' heard a word I've said Geordy?", Mary asked.

"Leave the lad alone, mither," William said. "He's just had his first taste of being a winner."

The next week at school was a different experience for George. There were no beatings and, in fact, his tormenters kept their distance from him, but from time to time there were flare ups and sometimes George was the instigator as his new-found confidence often bordered on arrogance. There were some boys who just wanted to test him, but he was ready for them. And his tongue could be sharp – a trait he had inherited from his grandmother Mary – but it got him out of many a scrape.

Mary was pleased that the fighting had stopped – or at least that George wasn't always on the bloodied nose end of a fight.

"Concentrate on your studies," was her nightly caution to George. "You can be or do anything you want," she would say as his confidence as a man grew. But he was headstrong, like her, and she knew that he would make his own decisions. She just hoped that they would be good decisions.

Chapter 48 (1912)

REMINISCING

In the Autumn of 1912, Mary was busy preparing for George's 15th birthday on November 16, and also for a family Christmas. She was 66 years old and the years were catching up with her. She was slower to move and after walking even a short distance she had begun to experience shortness of breath. There were times when she became anxious, often after she had been reminiscing about her life and her family, as she often did now. Her son William, now 30, and her grandson George were still the only family she had left and they were the light of her life.

As she stood alone in the kitchen of the little house at Barhill Road, and mixed the batter for the cake she was making for George's birthday, she thought about the cakes and buns that her sons Douglas and Andrew had often brought home from the bakery where they worked. She thought about how her daughter Janey used to be at her side helping in the kitchen and looking after her older brothers and the little ones. Ah, the little ones – the two wee Margarets and Andrew – who didn't even live long enough to know life. She was saddened to think that just a few years ago the Glen Afton Sanitorium for people with tuberculosis had been built closeby in New Cumnock. She didn't know then, and perhaps the doctors didn't know either, that the disease was spread by coughing and sneezing, and that it was exacerbated by living in damp and cramped quarters. Perhaps her children may have had a chance if the Sanitorium had been built when they were sick. Perhaps Douglas would have lived to know his boy, George, and the second Andrew would have married and had children.

She thought of her son Thomas and his dear friend Keir Hardie who had devoted much of his life to improve wages and conditions for miners. Would Thomas still be alive if the improvements in the mines, though minimal, had been introduced before he contracted Miners Phthisus like his father.

Of her eight children, Douglas was the only one to present her with a grandchild and she cherished young George, with both a grandmother's and a mother's love, for the boy had needed a mother when his own mother Agnes died so soon after his birth, and Mary needed a child in her life.

She brought herself back to the present and poured the cake batter into a tin ready for the oven. She wanted to make this a special birthday celebration for George. At 15 he was eligible to leave school and start a job but she wanted to keep him in school as long as she could and was actively looking for an apprenticeship for him.

And William. She would like to see him settled with a nice lass and start to produce more grandchildren. But William would do things in his own time. He was just like his father.

It was November 16, George's birthday, and the nights were drawing in. He didn't want any friends over – he thought he was a bit too old for that – so it was just George, his grandmother Mary and his uncle William who sat down together for their evening meal to be followed by the much looked-forward-to fruit cake. There was no family to invite – they were all gone – it was just the three of them.

After supper was over and the candles blown out on the cake, George asked his grandmother, as he did every birthday, to tell him about his parents, Agnes and Douglas.

"Oh Geordy," she began as she cut the cake, "you were such a special baby. Your mother was fearful sick with the consumption or tuberculosis as they called it, but she gave birth to a good, strong lad and held on for three months before God called her home. And your father, so proud he was of you and so sick himself and all. He walked with you every night when you fussed and couldn't wait to get home from work at the bakery to take you in his arms. Then he lost his battle with the consumption, and so did your uncle Andrew, and it was just the three of us, and is now."

She finished putting the cake on plates and handing them around. "Now come on Geordy, eat your cake."

"Aye, gran, it looks as good as always," George said. "But this year, I'd like to say something." He put down his fork and sat back in his chair.

"I'm almost a man and I feel the time has come to speak as a man," he said as he straightened his back. "I'm awfully grateful to you gran and uncle Will for raisin' me. I hope I've not been too much of a bother to ye, but, well, that's all I'd like to say, and that's my thoughts." He picked up his fork and began to eat the cake.

Mary looked across at William and smiled. They'd done a good job with the boy and he could speak for himself. Mary was happy.

After his 15th birthday, George reluctantly stayed on at school and Mary planned another Christmas celebration. It seemed that everything she did these days reminded her of times past. She thought of Christmases past, and the stockings hung by the fire and how she'd often struggled to find something to put in them for when her children woke on Christmas morning.

Two days before Christmas, she set off down the road with a basket over her arm to buy fresh fowl and vegetables and some treats for 'her boys'.

"Good morning Mrs McMurdo," said Old Brown the greengrocer. "And what can I fetch fer ye today?"

Mary reached into her basket for her shopping list and felt a pain shoot up her left arm. She dropped the basket and started to fall on the shop floor, but Old Brown was quick off the mark and he caught her before she reached the floorboards.

"Get some smelling salts," Old Brown called to his wife who came quickly with the ammonia-smelling bottle. She waved it under Mary's nose and she came to with a cough.

"Are you all right Mrs McMurdo?," asked Old Brown, but Mary could not speak. "Fetch the doctor wife," barked Old Brown. The doctor arrived in his horse and cart, examined Mary then, with the help of Old Brown, carried her to his cart and took her home. Old Brown's wife went to the school to fetch young George and he sat with his grandmother until William returned from work.

"It's just a bit of a turn," she said to them both. "Nothing to worry about."

But the doctor called William aside.

"Your mother is showing signs of Arterio Sclerosis. She came to see me about 12 months ago complaining of shortness of breath and chest pain and I feared a problem then. It's her heart," the doctor said.

"But she's never said a word," William said in shock.

"She's a strong, proud woman. She didn't want anyone fussing over her, but she'll have to take it easy now. That's doctor's orders," the doctor said.

"Aye, we'll see to that," said William.

They had a quiet Christmas with Mary confined to bed on her son's orders and the neighbour Mrs Hodge cooking the fowl, vegetable and pudding for a basic Christmas dinner. William tried to make the day as pleasant as possible, for he knew that this could be his mother's last Christmas.

Chapter 49 (1913)

THE END OF AN ERA

The winter snow piled up against the door of the little house at Barhill Road as George and William kept the fire stoked and the two-roomed house cosy and warm. The neighbours brought in food and Mrs Hodge next door came and tidied up most days. But Mary hated all the fuss and, although she grew ever weaker, she resented other people taking over her house.

"Will you stop all the fuss," she would say to anyone who dropped by. "I can make do for myself." But the truth was that the most she could do each day was get out of bed and tend to her personal needs before collapsing into the chair by the fire where she spent most of her days. She tried valiantly to cook a meal and tidy the house, even venturing out in the snow on more than one occasion, trying to get to the shops but inevitably she would make it just a few doors away then lean on a neighbour's wall until someone would find her and bring her home.

She battled through the winter with shortness of breath and chest pains, but as the snow gave way to the first blades of grass in the Spring she began to feel better. She would sit on a chair in the weak sunlight and watch the people of the village go about their work and leisure. She'd never been one for gossip, but these days she knew everyone's business, simply because she had the time to watch the passing parade.

On a July afternoon, as she sat warming herself in the early Summer sun, she heard the siren go off up at the mine. Whenever there was a cave-in, flooding or explosion at a mine, the siren sounded to advise families that there was an emergency and to let off-duty miners know that they were needed at the mine to help with the rescue attempt. George was still at school at his grandmother's insistence, although he would rather have been working, and William was on the day shift.

Mary rose from her chair, clutching at her chest.

"William," was all she said. She watched friends and neighbours rushing by, all heading for the mine. She weakly called out to one of the off-duty coal miners as he ran past.

"Mr McLatchey, what's happened?," she asked with her arm outstretched.

"A cave-in, it looks like Mrs McMurdo. All the lads are heading up there now," McLatchey said.

"My Will," she cried. "My Will."

"Aye, I'll look for him mysel'. Don't fret," he said as he called to his wife.

"Take Mrs McMurdo inside the hoose," he said and his wife took Mary gently by the arm into the house and made her a cup of tea.

At the mine, there was a flurry of activity up top as plans were put into action for the rescue. Ten men were trapped down below – and William was one of them.

The rescue team was made up of volunteers who knew the mine. They knew that it was nearing the end of the day shift when many of the miners had already left the mine, that a loud noise was heard. As about 25 men were nearing the entrance to the shaft, they looked back and saw a cloud of smoke chasing them. After a quick tally when they reached the surface, they knew that 10 men had been left behind, trapped by the falling coal and rubble.

McLatchey arrived on the scene to offer his expert knowledge of the mine and his intimate experience with cave-ins – he had been trapped himself at the same mine just five years before.

The deputy already had the mine maps laid out on a table and the last men out of the mine were pinpointing where they thought the coal fall had taken place.

"There's a pocket of air closeby that should last them several hours," McLatchey said. "If we try to approach from on top, and dig down, we'll get to them by nightfall."

Heartened by this positive news, the men gathered together their picks and shovels and an area was cordoned off for the men to work in.

News was relayed back to the village where women and children waited and prayed.

McLatchey's wife went outside of Mary's house to hear the latest news and came back inside.

"There are ten men trapped underground and William is among them," she said. "But they have air and the men are digging down now to free them."

"Oh William, my only remaining child," Mary said out loud. "You must live, you must." Then burying her head in her hands and turning her attention to God, she prayed: "Dear God, have I not sacrificed enough. You've taken seven of my eight children, now please don't take my last. You'll have me soon enough, please be happy with that. Let my William live." She didn't cry and Mrs McLatchey didn't understand why.

"I've cried a million tears over the years, Mrs McLatchey," she began by way of explanation. "Have you ever buried a child, Mrs McLatchey? Have you ever had your baby die in your arms, or watched your adult child waste away before your eyes, knowing that there is nothing that you can do? Or seen your husband spit up black phlegm from years working in a coal mine, only to see him gasp for his last breath?"

Mary paused to take a sip of her tea, then continued on weakly.

"Each time I lost one of my family, a little piece of my heart was buried with them, and the little bit of heart I had left became hard as a stone. That's why I cannot cry Mrs McLatchey, for the old shrivelled hard heart I have left is letting me down and it will be the death of me." Turning her attention back to her prayers, she said: "God, if you have to take someone this night, take me and let my William live."

Mary slumped at the table and Mrs McLatchey lead her to bed and tucked her in, then went outside to see if there was any further news. George was now home and keeping watch over his grandmother.

By 7pm, the men were freed and all were alive. William was carried home on a stretcher, with two broken ribs and a deep gash on his left leg which the doctor cleaned and stitched, then bound his chest. Mrs McLatchey bathed William's face and arms and legs and he asked about his mother.

"She's failing," Mrs McLatchey warned. William lifted himself from the chair by the fire and hobbled to his mother's bedside. He sat down on the bed, gently took her hand and winced at the pain from his broken ribs.

"I'm here mither," he whispered. Mary's skin was grey and her breathing shallow. She opened her eyes and saw the face of her son and smiled weakly.

"Will," was all that she could say. She squeezed his hand. "My son, you are here. I've been having such dreams about your father and your brothers and sisters. They were here, in the room with me."

William looked across at Mrs McLatchey, who just shook her head. George was in the kitchen, sitting at the table with his head in his hands. Seeing his uncle William injured and his gran so seriously ill was taking a toll on the boy.

"Will," Mary said softly. "You've to promise me something." She paused as she struggled for breath. "You're not to let our George go down the mines. Promise me now."

William had made a promise to his dying brother Douglas that he would look after his infant son, and he had kept that promise and raised the child as though he was his own.

But now the boy was 15 and almost old enough to make up his own mind. Could he make a promise to his dying mother that he may not be able to keep?

"I don't want that boy down a coal mine and another woman worrying herself sick about whether he'll come home or not. Do you hear me son?"

"I hear ye mither," William said. "I've done a good job of looking after the boy so far, have I not?," he asked.

"Aye, and a grand job at that," Mary said.

"Then you must trust me to continue to look after the boy and when he is a man he must make his own decisions," William said, afraid to make a promise that he could not keep.

"He's a good lad – all I ask is that you look out for him. He's also my grandson and he'll do what he thinks best, nothing surer," she said as a faint smile crossed her lips.

Exhausted, Mary closed her eyes and struggled for every breath. She had lived a busy and traumatic life and she was worn out. William summoned George to Mary's bedside and told him to say his goodbyes.

"Your gran is going to meet your grandpa, your mither and faither, and your aunts and uncles and she needs us to be happy about that," William told the boy.

It was hard for George to understand about this place where all the people he loved had to go, and he was angry, but he gently stroked his grandmother's grey hair and kissed her lined forehead, before dissolving into tears and leaving the room.

William, although in agony from his injuries, sat by his mother's bed throughout the night. At six minutes past 1am on July 31, 67-year-old Mary Percy Hamilton McMurdo drew her last breath, and at last her brave heart was at peace. It was the end of an era – a time of heartache, poverty, illness, death and sacrifice – and she had lived through it all with courage and grace.

William touched her hand and gazed into his mother's care-worn face. The wrinkles, gained from years of worry and heartache, seemed to have softened and there was a peacefulness about her. She had finally been released from the pain that had been a major part of most of her married life.

The body that had given life to eight children and cared for them all when they were sick and dying, was worn out and thin, but there was still a strength about her.

Her long struggle on earth had ended. She had done her best.

Chapter 50 (1913)

THE FAMILY LEGACY

Mary was laid to rest at the Muirkirk cemetery, in the family plot with the headstone that she had saved so hard for to have made, and her name was added to the long list of McMurdo names.

She had been an exceptionally strong woman, of enormous fortitude and courage who carried herself with pride and spoke her mind. She nursed her family through illness, had her heart broken over and over, but picked herself up and carried on.

After the funeral, William and George returned to the little house on Barhill Road. The place was empty without her. As William set about making a pot of tea, George sat down at the table.

"What do we do now Uncle Will?," he asked sadly.

"Well, it's just we two bachelors now Geordy. What do ye think we should do?"

"I know one thing's for certain," George said. "I'll no' be going back to the school. Do ye think you can get me a job with you in the pits?," he asked.

"Now Geordy, you know yer gran's feelings about that..."

George cut him off mid-sentence. "Aye, I do, but did ye no feel pride when you started in the pits – feeling that you were carrying on a proud family tradition? Well, that's what I want too. To work side by side with you and to be the strong man that gran wanted me to be. And I'll do it," George concluded sternly with a light thump of his fist on the table.

William poured them both a cup of tea, then sat down at the table beside his nephew.

"Well, it seems you certainly have the McMurdo fire in your blood, Geordy, and there's no arguing with a McMurdo once he's made up his mind."

George took a gulp on the tea, and looked at his uncle.

"It's no' easy work mind, and you'll be tired and sore at the end of the day, but if it's what you want, I can get you started on Monday," William said.

"It's what I want Uncle Will, more than anything." And so it was settled.

On Monday morning, young George packed a sandwich in his piece-box, took down his new cloth cap from the peg by the door, and closed the door on the little house in Barrhill Road before proudly walking beside his uncle on the way to the colliery.

And in his mind, though he'd never met them, he imagined the coal-stained faces of his grandfather George and his great-grandfather Thomas, his Uncle Thomas and Keir Hardie, in their pit clothes walking along beside them. The lad had only ever known his grandmother Mary and his Uncle William, but they kept alive the stories of his parents, grandparents, aunts and uncles, and young George could feel their loving embrace with each step he took towards the mines. He was a colliery man now and he would carry on the work and the proud tradition of the McMurdo men who had gone before him.

***

END NOTE

The two men, uncle and nephew, remained together in the house in Barrhill Road for the next 10 years, but they did get a housekeeper – and therein lies another story.

SCOTTISH WORDS

Aboot – About
Afeared – Afraid
Aw – All
Aye – Yes

Bonnie - Beautiful
Box bed – A pine bed built into the wall of a house to save space
Braw – Fine/good

But'n'Ben – Two roomed house (But – livingroom/kitchen
Ben – Bedroom

Cannae – Cannot
Cavel – A share of property, assigned lot

Deid – Dead
Dinnae – Don't
Doilies - Small mats or cloths, often crocheted, placed under ornaments
Doesnae – Does not
Doon – Down
Dram – Small measure of whisky
Drap – Drop

Een - Eyes

Faither – Father
Fash – Trouble/bother
Fathom – Unit of depth = 1.8 metres
Frae – From
Feet – Measurement: 1 foot = 30cm
Fer – For

Halfpenny – Half a penny
Hame – Home
Heed – Mind
Heid – Head
Hissel' – Himself
Hoose – House

Inches – Measurement: 1 inch = 2.5cm

Jeely piece – Jam sandwich

Kirkyard - Churchyard

Midden – Dunghill
Mither – Mother

Mort cloth – Hired from church to cover deceased
Muir - Moorland

Neeps – Turnips
Nay – No
Neb – Nose
Neeps - Turnips
No' - Not

Och – Oh
Oor – Our
Oot – Out
Ounce – Unit of weight

Pence - Pennies
Pie-eyed - Drunk
Piece box – Miner's Lunchbox
Pounds – Currency: 20 shillings; weight = 16 ounces (about 500g)

Shilling – Currency: (AUS) 10 cents; (UK) 10p; (US) 10 cents
Shooders – Shoulders
Sook – Suck
Sourpuss – Grumpy person
Sweeties – Lollies; candy

Tak – Take
Tatties - Potatoes
Telt - Told

Weans – Children
Wee – Small
Wi' - With

Yards – Unit of measurement = .91 metre
Ye – You
Yer – Your

24793604R00109

Printed in Great Britain
by Amazon